Mail Order Mirth
Book 48 in Brides of Beckham
Kirsten Osbourne

Copyright © 2023 by Kirsten Osbourne

Unlimited Dreams Publishing

All rights reserved.

Cover design by Erin Dameron Hill/ EDH Graphics

No part of this book may be reproduced in any form or by any electronic or mechanical means including information storage and retrieval systems, without permission in writing from the author. The only exception is by a reviewer, who may quote short excerpts in a review.

This book is a work of fiction. Names, characters, places, and incidents either are products of the author's imagination or are used fictitiously. Any resemblance to actual persons, living or dead, events, or locales is entirely coincidental.

Kirsten Osbourne

Visit my website at www.kirstenandmorganna.com

Chapter One

Amelia Beckham had just finished school, and she knew she needed to find something to do with her life. There were different factories she could work in, but factories and manufacturers all seemed so dark and grim. And Amelia was sunshine on a stick. She loved the world and the people around her. She wished she could take all the people of the world into her arms to keep them safe.

As an orphan who had been left at the Beckham Orphanage in Beckham, Massachusetts as an infant, she had less time to make up her mind than others did, but surely there was a place for someone who had never met a person she hadn't liked in the world. She considered every stranger a future friend.

She had one month to decide what to do before she had to leave the orphanage forever. Most children had to leave as soon as they finished school, but Amelia was known for brightening everyone's day, making the small children easier to manage.

Amelia walked into the store. She didn't have any money to spend, but that was all right. She simply loved being around people, and the store would have people.

Once inside, she wandered around the big general store. She looked at the different fabrics, imagining how lovely it would be to have new clothes to wear instead of the patched donation clothing that the orphanage received.

She stopped in front of the bulletin board, surprised she'd never seen it before. Perhaps there would be a job or a room for rent. Hopefully, both because if she didn't have a job, she couldn't pay rent on the room. Oh, it seemed like such a glorious opportunity. She was sure there would be something there for her!

As she looked over the different notices, she found someone who was looking for a mother's helper, which sounded like a truly glorious job, but it only paid fifteen cents per day, and she wouldn't be able to afford a place to stay.

She kept looking, and finally she came across an ad for mail-order brides. What a wonderful idea! She could brighten up a lonely man's life, and she knew she would find true love. How could she not? She liked everyone, and she was certain everyone liked her. How could they not? She was a dose of pure sunshine to brighten any day.

She looked at the ad again to get the address to report to, and she left the store, walking the short distance to Rock Creek Road, to talk to Elizabeth Tandy. Everyone in town knew of the Tandys as they were one of the wealthiest families around, but Amelia had never had the pleasure of meeting Mrs. Tandy, who was said to be a wonderful person. She knew they'd get along because she got along with everyone.

She walked to the door and boldly knocked, a smile on her face for whomever came to the door. A tall blond man was there, and Amelia looked up at him. "Hello. I'm here to see Elizabeth Tandy about becoming a mail-order bride. I cannot wait to move to the West and bless a man with my presence."

He opened the door wide for her to step inside. "Your name, miss?"

"I'm Miss Amelia Beckham," she said proudly.

The man nodded, taking her to the last door on the left, and opening the door. "Elizabeth, I have a young woman here who would like to be a mail-order bride."

Elizabeth stood. "Come in!"

Amelia walked in, and when the man didn't introduce her, she introduced herself. "Hello! I'm Amelia Beckham, and I'd like to be a mail-order bride. I imagine the journey this will take me on will be one I remember for the rest of my life. Do you usually send brides on trains or stagecoach? I think I'd rather take a train because I've never been on one."

Mrs. Tandy smiled. "Usually by train. Have a seat."

Amelia sat down on the sofa across from Mrs. Tandy's desk. "I do hope you have someone who is willing to receive a bride soon. I only have a month before I have to leave the orphanage, and I would like to not have to move twice. Of course, I have nowhere to move here, but that's neither here nor there."

"I do think I have someone for you. How do you feel about hot summers?"

"Oh, they're glorious. I can swim and garden and just be outdoors."

"All right. First, how old are you?"

"I'm eighteen, and I just finished all my schooling yesterday, so I can read, write, do arithmetic, and I'm quite handy in the kitchen and I love to clean. Oh, this opportunity is what I've waited my whole life for!"

Elizabeth smiled. "All right. Then let me give you this letter."

Dear Prospective Bride,

I hope this letter finds you well. I write this under the dim glow of my lantern in the late hours of the Texas night. My name is Anthony, And I'm a man of thirty who has experienced much more than his fair share of life's bitter truths.

Life has dealt me a harsh hand, leaving me a widower with two young sons to raise on my own. Samuel is six and Ethan is barely four; both are as rambunctious as young colts. They are the light in my otherwise dreary existence, their laughter echoing in our humble home nestled amidst the vast wilderness.

Now, I won't sugarcoat my words or paint a picture prettier than it is. Life here is tough, the work is hard, and leisure is a luxury we can seldom afford. But it's a living, and it's the only one I've got to offer.

My wife's absence has left a void in our lives, particularly in areas that I, as a man, oftentimes, find myself ill-equipped to handle. I need a woman's touch in my house, someone who can manage our humble home, prepare meals for my boys, and keep things clean.

Now, I may come across as gruff and perhaps a bit too straightforward, but I believe in honesty. Besides companionship, I seek physical intimacy that only a wife can provide. It's been far too long since I've known the warmth of a woman, and I yearn for that closeness again.

I make no grand promises of undying love. I am a simple man with simple needs. But I promise you a stable life, a roof over your head, and a place in our small family.

If you are a woman of strength, not afraid to roll up her sleeves and face the challenges of frontier life, I encourage you to respond. Perhaps together, we can carve out a decent life in this wild land.

I eagerly await your response.

Sincerely,

Anthony

As Amelia read the letter, she could imagine just how much joy she could bring to Anthony and his children. "He's perfect! May I write him back?"

Elizabeth pushed a piece of paper, a pen, and an inkwell toward the girl, watching her as she wrote her letter of response.

Dearest Anthony,

The words of your letter are resonating in my heart. It is a quiet day here in Massachusetts, and as I pen these words to you, I am filled with a sense of hope and anticipation.

My name is Amelia, and though I am but eighteen summers old, life has taught me lessons far beyond my years. I am an orphan who has never known her family. Yet, I have always found joy in the smallest of things - the rustle of leaves in the wind, the laughter of my friends at the orphanage, the simple pleasure of a warm meal. I have learned to embrace life with all its challenges and celebrate its small victories.

The honesty in your words, the rawness of your needs, the promise of a new beginning - it all beckons me toward you and your little ones.

I may not have the experience of managing a household of my own, but what I lack in experience, I make up for in enthusiasm and a willingness to learn. I can cook, clean, and most importantly, I can care. I can be the nurturing presence your boys need, the companion you seek.

The thought of physical intimacy is indeed daunting to a young woman like me. However, I trust that you, being a man of more experience, will guide me with patience and kindness. Together, we can explore this aspect of our relationship with mutual respect and understanding.

Anthony, I assure you, I am not one to shy away from hard work or challenges. The promise of a life filled with honest work, shared responsibilities, and the companionship of a family is more than an orphan like me could ever dream of.

I am ready to embark on this journey with you, to share in your days, to be a part of your family. I hope that my words bring you comfort and a sense of anticipation for our shared future.

I await your reply with bated breath and a hopeful heart.

Yours sincerely,

Amelia

As she signed her name with a flourish, Amelia knew that she was doing the right thing. This man and his children needed her, and she couldn't wait to be right there with them, ready to take on the world as part of a family and not just some lost orphan.

"I'll get this mailed off in the morning. If you don't mind, I'll suggest he respond by telegram so we can get you off to Texas before your thirty-day deadline is up."

"What a wonderful idea! Will someone tell me when you've received his response?"

"I'll send my husband to tell you. He's the one who answered the door." There was a soft knock at the door, and Mr. Tandy came inside the room, carrying a tray of cookies and lemonade. "Please stay and share a treat with me."

Amelia smiled and nodded. "We don't get sweet treats often at the orphanage. The matron is always worried we'll have to have our teeth seen to."

"I see." Elizabeth poured them each a glass of lemonade, and she put two cookies on each of the two plates provided. "Tell me, Amelia. Do you have any Sunday dresses?"

Amelia looked down for a moment. "No, I don't. This is my only dress. Should I have something nicer to go to Texas?"

Elizabeth frowned. "I have some fabric here that was given to me by a young lady who was about to go West to marry. She had more than anyone could possibly need and said I should use what's left for someone who could use it."

"And you're going to let me have it? Oh, Mrs. Tandy, that is the most wonderful charitable thing I've ever seen anyone do. Thank you so much! I don't care if it's the ugliest color in the world. I'll wear it with pride."

Elizabeth smiled. "I think the fabric will suit you nicely." She stood and went to one corner of her office and opened a trunk. "There's this..." She held up a pink with little flowers all over it. Then she held up a white fabric. "There's some white lace in here as well. Perhaps you can make a wedding dress from it that will double as your Sunday dress."

"I love it. Oh, thank you!"

With a smile, Elizabeth pulled out a soft blue fabric. "This will be beautiful with your eyes."

Amelia couldn't help but clap her hands together with excitement. "I love them all! I should be able to finish three dresses within a month. Oh, thank you, Mrs. Tandy. You're changing my life, and I couldn't be happier!"

"I'm happy to do all I can to prepare you for the journey. I think there's also some white muslin in here if you want to make yourself a new nightgown and maybe even an apron."

"I would love to. I don't even know how to thank you properly!"

"Your smile is thanks enough," Elizabeth said, vowing to herself to buy more fabric to replace what she was giving. There were so many brides who needed clothes before they could go.

Amelia finished her cookies and stood up, accepting the fabric. "I need to go get to work!" she said, excitedly. "I have plans for my future and fabric for pretty dresses. It's like my whole world changed for the better when I saw your advertisement at the store."

"I'll be in touch as soon as we know something," Mrs. Tandy promised. "Sew quickly."

Amelia practically skipped all the way to the orphanage. The girls were in one large room and the boys in another. There was a parlor for quiet play or work, and a kitchen. There was a single bedroom downstairs where the matron stayed. Everyone else who worked at the orphanage was a volunteer.

She hurried straight to the kitchen, where the matron was cooking their supper. "Mrs. Mitchell. Mrs. Mitchell!"

Mrs. Mitchell turned with a look of annoyance along with a look of humor. "Yes?"

"I'm going to Texas to be a mail-order bride! And Mrs. Tandy gave me enough fabric to make myself three new dresses, a nightgown, and even an apron."

Mrs. Mitchell looked relieved. "Oh, that is wonderful news!"

"I'm so excited! And I'll use as little fabric as possible, and perhaps there will be enough left for a dress or two for the little ones."

"You always think of others, which is one of my favorite things about you," Mrs. Mitchell said. She'd been at the orphanage for three years, and while at first, she'd seemed annoyed at how excited about everything Amelia tended to be, she had grown to love her.

Amelia hurried to the parlor and took advantage of the needle and thread Mrs. Mitchell kept there for the girls' convenience. First, she cut out the dress, and then she began sewing. Amelia loved to sew, and she always helped with the mending. There was enough fabric from the first dress for another girl her size. Now she had to sew even faster, so she could finish a dress for her friend, Heidi, who had always shared a room with her.

She sewed until supper and then helped with the dishes, which was one of her chores for the week, before she went back to sewing.

Three weeks later, when Mr. Tandy came to give her the train ticket for her trip to Texas, all the dresses were done, as well as her new nightgown and an apron that would completely cover the front of her dress.

She had been able to make seven dresses total out of the fabric and two nightgowns. Sharing her good fortune was something Amelia never forgot to do. She was happy to help out the other orphans, and would have been happy to help someone else as well.

She accepted the ticket, realizing she was leaving on the morning train, and in a few short days, she'd be in Texas, ready to take on the world as a wife and mother. Could life be any better?

Chapter Two

When Amelia arrived in Midland, Texas, and stood on the train platform waiting for her Anthony, she stood looking in every direction. She was exhausted because she hadn't slept her best on the train, but that wasn't going to stop her from being happy to meet her new family.

She wore one of her new dresses, and it was wrinkled beyond what an iron would fix. She would need to wash it and hang it up before it would look like a dress again.

Anthony Martin sat in his wagon, looking at the only woman on the train platform. She was a pretty young thing with blonde hair and blue eyes, looking as if she was ready to take on the world. Her dress, while wrinkled, was a pretty pink with small flowers all over it. She looked much too young to be the mother of his children, but his mother had taught him many years before that beggars can't be choosers.

After a moment, he got down from his wagon and walked to her. He tipped his cowboy hat and said, "Amelia?"

Her whole face lit up when she heard his deep voice. He was much taller than her, but everyone was, and he had dark hair with dark brown eyes. He was very tanned. "Yes, I'm Amelia! It's so good to meet you. You must be Anthony. Did you bring the boys?"

Anthony shook his head. "No, I left them with my foreman's wife. She's the one who watches them during the day."

"But she won't have to now because I'm here. Oh, I can't wait to meet them."

He leaned down and picked up her small bag that held every belonging she'd ever had, and walked quickly to the wagon. For a moment she didn't think he would remember to help her up, but he came back and offered his hand to her.

No one had ever helped her into a wagon before, and she was thrilled to be marrying a man who was chivalrous. He was perfect in every way. Oh, he was a bit intimidating, but she'd get over that. "Are we marrying straight away?" she asked. She hoped there would be time for her to change into the dress she'd made to be married in.

He nodded. "Pastor is waiting on us. I'm glad your train was on time because I need to get back out to the ranch as soon as I can. A few of our herd ended up on a neighbor's land last night, and my men and I are doing our best to find them all."

Without asking, she knew the answer would be no if she asked for time to clean up and change clothes, but that was fine. If he'd only seen her as she was, he would be more impressed to see her later. "So you're a rancher?"

He nodded. "I'm a rancher and a fourth generation Texan. My great-grandfather died at the Alamo," he said.

She wasn't certain why he sounded so proud to tell her how his great-grandfather had died, but she smiled and nodded. "I've never even been out of Beckham, Massachusetts before this."

He nodded. "You'll find that even though we Texans are Americans as well, we have our own identity. Having been our own republic for a time makes us mighty proud to be who we are."

"Tell me about your boys," she said. She couldn't wait to meet them and love them and feed them. Oh, being a mother must be the best thing in the whole wide world.

He nodded. "Samuel will be seven by the time school starts, so he'll start attending our small country school in September. Ethan is pretty quiet. He's a good kid, but he misses his mother almost as much as I do."

"How did your wife die, if you don't mind my asking?"

He minded. But he felt she needed to know about him and his boys. "She got sick, and by the time I got home with the doctor, she was gone. Doc thinks it was Russian Flu, but without her being alive to question, he's not sure. She died in February, and I will always miss her."

"Of course, you will!" she said, expecting nothing less from him.

"You won't mind if I talked to the kids about her then?" he asked.

"Of course, you should. Tell me about her, and I'll talk to them about her too. If not for her, we couldn't be forming a family now."

He gave her a strange look as he stopped the wagon. Helping her down, he went to a small house behind a church. "Parsonage is back here. Pastor is expecting us."

Amelia nodded, following him to the church. "I was raised in a church-run orphanage," she said. "It was lovely there. We always had friends to play with and things to do. Even chores were fun when we were doing them with friends."

"Did all the orphans feel that way, or just you?" he asked. He'd never heard of an orphan who had loved their life in the orphanage. Without waiting for her to answer, he knocked on the door.

"Probably just me. But I loved it there. I can't think of a better way for children to grow up."

He nodded. "All right." She'd clearly lost her mind, and he was marrying a crazy woman. He just hoped she could really cook and clean. Maybe her insanity was a type that could be treated.

The pastor's wife came to the door, smiling. "Do you have time for your bride to freshen up a little?" she asked Anthony.

He shook his head. "I'm afraid I don't. We lost some of our herd last night, and I need to be with my men hunting them down just as soon as I can be."

She patted his hand. "The life of a rancher." She swung the door wide. "Come in! I'll get Bob."

Pastor Bob's wife scurried away to get her husband, leaving Anthony and Amelia in awkward silence. "How long is the drive to the ranch?" Amelia asked. She hated to hear only quiet around her. She hoped she'd have a lot of friends nearby when they did get there.

"Only about an hour," he said. "We have a school and a church there, so we don't always have to drive into town, but I wanted us to be married as soon as possible." He was still half-convinced she'd change her mind. Who would agree to be a wife to a man who lived so far from the nearest town?

Pastor Bob came in, straightening his tie. "I appreciate you stopping by on the way to the train station to let me know you'd be coming for a wedding."

Anthony nodded. "Seemed only right."

The wedding was incredibly short and very simple. To Amelia it felt as if the whole world opened up when they spoke their vows, but Anthony seemed unmoved. That was all right though. She'd teach him.

Instead of kissing her mouth, he kissed her cheek, which was a bit disappointing until Amelia realized they would have their first kiss in private, where it would be so much more romantic than a forced kiss in front of strangers.

As they walked back to the wagon, she felt as if she was too happy to walk on the ground. Her feet were on the air instead. He helped her back into the wagon. "I picked up some supplies before I went to the train station," he told her. "You should have all the basics. If you need me to purchase more, just let me know."

"Is the closest store here in Midland?" she asked.

"Yup."

"How did Midland get its name?" she asked. "Do you know?" Surely that would have him talking more. She loved hearing his voice, which was low and almost gravelly.

"I do. Midland was established in 1881 as the midpoint between Fort Worth and El Paso, both of which are important Texas cities. They called it Midway for a bit but when we got our first post office here, they changed the name to Midland because there are already other cities called Midway in Texas."

"Have you lived here long?" she asked.

He shook his head. "I was raised not far outside of Fort Worth, but there was free land for the taking out here, so I started my ranch here. Moved in 1890."

"That makes sense. Was your father a rancher?"

"Yup."

"Have you always wanted to follow in his footsteps?" she asked, trying to keep him talking.

"Yup. Pa was one of the most prominent ranchers in the area, and he told me if I wanted to ranch, he'd start me out with one-hundred head of cattle. With money I'd saved over the years, I hired two men, and the three of us drove them from Pa's ranch to here. I'll never forget that he gave me my start."

"That's really good that he helped you out so much. Your first wife, did you meet her here?"

"Mary? Yup. I saw her in church the first Sunday I was here, and we started courting right after that. Took me two years to convince her pa she needed to marry me, but he finally agreed."

"What do the boys like to do?" Amelia asked.

"Oh, usual boy stuff. They like to run around outside, often with no clothes on. They like to eat."

She smiled. "There were three boys in my orphanage, and they would always strip off their clothes and run around outside. The matron would always send me out to get them. Not because they listened to me any better than they listened to her, but because I would laugh. I think it's glorious to be so uninhibited that you can run around with nothing on."

"I hope you don't run around that way," he said, frowning at her.

She shrugged. "Never have, but I may try it someday soon."

"I would rather you didn't."

"All right then. I'll just bring our sons in after they've run around naked."

He was surprised to hear her say "our" in regard to his children. How did she already think they were hers? This girl was a bit of a mystery to him. He wasn't sure if he wanted it to stay that way.

"Has your foreman's wife been watching them every day since Mary died?"

"Every day but Sunday, when I get them all to myself. Sundays are disasters waiting to happen. I have a housekeeper as well, but she takes her day off on Mondays so I at least don't have to cook on Sunday. I have to cook Monday, but at least I'm not worn out from chasing the boys all day."

"You cook?" she asked, surprised. Most men didn't cook, and wouldn't admit it if they did.

He nodded. "Only when it's necessary," he replied. "I can ruin anything without even trying."

"I love to cook. We all took turns cooking with the matron and doing all the other chores. We'd have to cook for a week, and then we'd have a week of cleaning, and then a week of mending. I enjoyed all the chores, and I was always trading with the other girls who didn't enjoy their chores as much as I did."

He raised an eyebrow. "You enjoy chores."

"I don't see that there's any reason to dread doing something you're just going to have to do anyway, so I've embraced all my chores, and I let myself love them. Why not?"

He blinked a few times. "Maybe I'll introduce you to mending fences. All my men would be trading your chores for theirs."

She giggled. "I'd gladly learn! The more I know, the more valuable I am to those around me."

"Are you always so...happy?" he asked.

She nodded emphatically. "Why waste one moment of your life in despair? I choose to be happy every day."

"I'm afraid I'm the opposite, especially since Mary died. I'm more likely to tell you to stop smiling so much."

Amelia squeezed his hand with hers. "I won't stop though. I'm determined to be happy with everything I do. If the boys are sad, then I'll cheer them up with a little song or a cheery dance."

"And if it doesn't work?"

"Then I'll bake cookies, or whatever they've chosen as their favorite treats." She looked all around on the deserted road. "Is it too late in the season to start growing a kitchen garden?"

"Leslie, my foreman's wife, started one for us. She thought it would be a nice welcome home gift to my bride. The boys helped her." Anthony couldn't figure out what to think about Amelia. He'd never met anyone who was quite so happy in his life.

"Oh, good! Then I'll keep it up and harvest it, and maybe I can give her some of the food I put up in the fall to thank her for all she did for us."

"She's paid well. No need to give her gifts," he said.

"Maybe not a need, but I like to do for others. Don't you?"

"I like to get my work done so there's food on the table," he responded. "I work very long days."

"How many men work for you?" she asked, happy he would be working on the ranch, and she'd see him every night. The wives of his men didn't sound like they were as fortunate.

"Thirty, if you count the cook, who makes all the meals for them."

"Of course, I count the cook," she said. "Does he cook in your house?"

Anthony shook his head. "No, he has an outside kitchen he uses. He says it's easier to cook for a large group of people if you do it outside."

"I can see where that would be true. I just can't wait to get to your house and see the ranch. I'm almost upset that you have a housekeeper because I would have enjoyed giving it a good cleaning for you and the boys."

"I'm sure Mrs. Hamilton won't mind your help," he said.

"I hope not. I plan to make friends with her right away. Where does she live?"

"She has a small house on my property. It's easy for her to walk the short distance to the house, and she never has to stay home because of inclement weather that way."

"Is she married?" Amelia asked.

He shook his head. "She was a good friend of my mother, and her husband died about ten years back. When I was looking for a housekeeper, Ma suggested she would be the best choice, so I hired her."

Amelia was thrilled to know she wouldn't be alone on the vast plains. No way would she enjoy that.

Chapter Three

When they reached the ranch, Amelia couldn't wait to get inside the house to see it all. Her new life was finally beginning, and it was going to be perfect. Instead of waiting for Anthony to help her down, she jumped down and ran toward the house, opening the door and looking all around her.

Everything was neat and tidy, and something smelled wonderful. She followed the smell into the kitchen and smiled at the woman there. She was older, and a bit hunched over. "I'm Amelia!" she said.

Mrs. Hamilton jumped a bit. "Oh, hello. I'm Mrs. Hamilton, Mr. Martin's housekeeper."

"It's so good to meet you. Supper smells delicious," Amelia said. "What are you making?"

"The men's cook is making a few briskets for the men, so he's going to bring some meat over for us. I am making potato salad and baked beans to go with it."

"I can't wait to try it! Where are the boys?"

Mrs. Hamilton couldn't help but smile then. "They're with Leslie, the foreman's wife. If you can give me a minute to wash my hands, I'll walk you over and introduce you."

Amelia clapped her hands. "Oh, I would adore that, Mrs. Hamilton. I've been dreaming of the day I would meet Anthony and his precious boys for almost a month, and I'm not sure I could wait another minute."

"I'm glad that you're excited. I must warn you that little Ethan is still very much in mourning for his mother. Nothing seems to cheer him up, even a little."

"That's so sad. I hope I can get him to smile soon."

"You seem like a very happy person," Mrs. Hamilton said to her.

"Oh, I am. I try to look at the bright side of everything that happens around me. When I can choose to be happy, there's no reason for sadness or anger," Amelia said, happy to see the woman was finished washing her hands and they could finally go and meet the boys.

Mrs. Hamilton led Amelia to the backdoor, and the two of them set out on the short walk to the foreman's house. Mrs. Hamilton pointed out as much as she could along the way. "The foreman's house is up in the distance," she said. "The boys may be playing outside, but it's most likely they're inside to try to escape the heat."

Amelia smiled. "I'll have to teach them to swim in the horse trough."

Mrs. Hamilton burst out laughing. "I'm not sure that's a great idea," she said. "It's not nearly deep enough to swim there, and water is scarce in these parts."

"I love your accent," Amelia said with a smile. "You sound just like someone from Texas should sound."

"I don't know about that, but I'm glad it pleases you." Mrs. Hamilton stopped for a moment. "Looks like the men found another of the lost calves," she said. "I don't know how they managed to get out."

"They probably just didn't know they were supposed to stay here, and there was land over there to explore," Amelia said, looking out to see the calf led back to the barn with a rope. "Don't they graze all summer?"

"Most do. But the calves need to stay close to the heifers to eat. And those went very far from their mothers. I hope we don't find out that someone deliberately took them or let them go. That wouldn't make Mr. Martin happy at all!"

"Does that happen?" Amelia asked.

"Oh, all the time, but it's never happened here. I'm probably worried for nothing."

As they got to the house, Mrs. Hamilton introduced Amelia to Leslie. "It's so good to meet you," Leslie said. "The boys are both napping, but I'll send them home as soon as they wake."

As much as she wanted to meet them immediately, she nodded. "That would be fine. I'm just very anxious to meet them and didn't want to wait."

Leslie laughed. "They'll be just the same but in a better mood when they wake," she said. "Ethan's having a bit of a hard day, so I hope that having a new mother will help him through that. I don't think Sam's really sleeping, but he lays down with Ethan often, so Ethan will rest better."

"It sounds like Sam is a wonderful big brother!" Amelia said, proud that Sam would be working so hard to help his brother.

Leslie shrugged. "He's a big brother. He helps when he can, and he picks on him the rest of the time. He thinks it's his job to make sure that Ethan does as he's told."

"I can't wait to meet them both. Thank you so much for sending them home when they wake."

"Do you think you'll start keeping them at home tomorrow?" Leslie asked.

Amelia nodded. "I do believe I will. I want to spend just as much time with them as I can." She nodded to Leslie's swollen stomach. "I'm sure you could use the rest before your little one is born."

Leslie smiled, patting her belly. "It's my first."

"Oh, I'm sure you'll love your baby just as much as I love Sam and Ethan. You'll understand when you're a mother." Amelia didn't notice the odd looks she was receiving from Mrs. Hamilton and Leslie. She was too busy talking about how much she loved her boys.

As they walked back to the house, Mrs. Hamilton smiled. "I hope we'll be able to get along with each other well. It will be so good to have someone here to help me."

"How did you and Mary split the chores?" Amelia asked, wanting to keep things close to the same as Mary had them because it was obvious her boys had enjoyed the way things had gone back then.

Mrs. Hamilton gave her an odd look. "She cooked suppers on my day off, and she tried to keep the house tidy while I was gone."

"But she didn't always tidy it?" Amelia felt badly for the dead woman. How hard it must have been for her to not be able to do all she wanted to do for her family.

"No, not always," Mrs. Hamilton said.

"I enjoy cooking and housework a great deal," Amelia said. "Are all the bedrooms upstairs?"

"Yes, of course."

"Then why don't I keep the upstairs and the bedrooms clean and tidy. I can help you cook, take care of the boys, and help sew for them of course. If I finish the upstairs before you get all your work done, I'll come down and do it. Do you cook breakfast, or do I?"

"I do."

"Then let me cook suppers. I cannot imagine never cooking. You have to let me have a turn!"

Mrs. Hamilton nodded. "Would you rather do breakfast? Then you can get the meal cooked before the boys are up, and they won't be underfoot."

"I could spend more time with the boys if I let you do supper, right?"

"I'm sure you'll get plenty of time with the boys either way," Mrs. Hamilton said. "They're a full-time job just the two of them."

"Then I'll take breakfast. And when the boys and I make something sweet in the kitchen, we'll clean up our own mess."

"It's hard to cook in the house in the summer," Mrs. Hamilton warned. "We have a fire pit outside I often use for roasting meat or making stews in summertime."

"Oh, that sounds very handy! Should I cook in that for breakfast?"

Mrs. Hamilton shook her head. "There's no need. As long as the windows are open most of the heat will dissipate from the house for breakfast. It's the other meals that are too hot."

When they got back to the house, Amelia noticed the bag with her belongings on the front porch. "You don't have to go up with me, but if you could tell me which room I'll share with Anthony, I'd appreciate it."

Mrs. Hamilton smiled. "I can go up the stairs with you."

"Oh, no need. I can explore and find the right room."

Amelia didn't wait for the older woman, but she sprang up the stairs and found what must be Anthony's room at the top of the stairs. She peeked in the other rooms to see the boys' beds made perfectly. She would have to start teaching them to make their own beds the very next day. In her experience boys did not make beds perfectly.

When she walked into Anthony's room, the bed looked so inviting. It had been almost a week since she'd slept in one, and that felt like forever. But instead of giving in to her tiredness, she put her bag on the bed and began unpacking it. Her dresses all needed to be ironed badly, so she didn't hang them in his wardrobe, but she put her brush on his dresser, and laid her nightgown on the bed, so it would be ready for her to put on when it was time.

She was a little nervous about sharing his bed with him, but he was a good man, which she'd already seen. She was certain her time with him would be nothing short of perfection. It was the type of man he was.

When she was finished, she took her other two dresses downstairs. "Would you mind telling me where the iron is?" Amelia asked. "I thought to change into one of my other dresses, but even though I packed them carefully, they are as wrinkled as the one I'm wearing."

"Oh, just set them down, and I'll take care of them," Mrs. Hamilton said.

Amelia laughed softly. "My hands do not need to be idle," she told the housekeeper. "I do much better when I'm busy."

"What happens when you're not busy?" Mrs. Hamilton asked.

"I start trying to fix the world," Amelia said sheepishly. "I'll find an injured animal, and do all I can to fix it. Or I'll see a couple who is unhappy, and I tell them what I love about each of them, usually annoying them. Or I'll decide to start a bake sale or something similar. Trust me, it's not a good idea."

Shaking her head, Mrs. Hamilton got the iron and ironing board out. "The stove is on, so you can just heat it there."

Amelia put the iron on the stove and set up the ironing board in the dining room, so she could still talk to Mrs. Hamilton as she worked. She stretched one of the dresses out onto the ironing board before sitting down while waiting for the iron to heat up.

"How long have you worked for Anthony?" Amelia called to Mrs. Hamilton.

"Ever since Mrs. Martin was expecting Sam. She thought she shouldn't have to do housework while she was with child, and Anthony gave in to her every whim."

"Oh," Amelia said, surprised. She'd never heard of a woman shirking her duties while she was expecting. "Did she have an especially difficult pregnancy?"

"Oh, no. Nothing like that."

Amelia wasn't sure what to think of her husband's first wife, but she refused to say a bad word about her. She'd decided long before that she wouldn't say bad things about anyone. Ever. It was one of the things that kept her joyful.

Mrs. Hamilton offered no more information on Anthony's first wife, and Amelia decided she would stop asking questions. No, it would be better if she envisioned the perfect mother for the boys.

She ironed both dresses before carrying them upstairs, and changing into the blue dress, which was her favorite of the ones she'd made. It fit perfectly, and she didn't have to wear a corset with it, which made it a perfect dress in her eyes.

When she went back downstairs, she put the ironing board and the iron away. "Is there a specific day of the week we should do laundry?" Amelia asked.

"I usually take care of it on Tuesdays," Mrs. Hamilton responded. "That's the day I have the most energy after taking Monday off."

Amelia nodded, smiling. "What day is it?" she asked.

Mrs. Hamilton laughed. "I suppose with as long as you were on that train, you'll have no idea what day of the week it is. Today is Friday."

"Anthony works on Saturdays?" Amelia asked.

"Anthony worked every day until Mary died, and he's only taken Sundays off since she's been gone. He always went to church, but he came right home and changed into his work clothes. He's a very hard-working man."

"All right. I'll keep that in mind." Amelia knew some women wouldn't like it if their husbands worked so much, but she felt that he had the right to do what he wanted with his time as long as he kept his family fed and clothed. He seemed like a very hard-working man to her.

"What can I do to help you with supper?" Amelia asked.

Mrs. Hamilton smiled. "It's all done. Unless you'd like to make some dinner rolls. The boys prefer their brisket on rolls, but I haven't taken the time to do them yet."

Amelia quickly washed her hands at the pump in the kitchen sink. "I would love to make rolls."

"It hurts my hands a lot to knead the dough, so I don't make bread as much as I used to."

"Then that'll be one of my chores," Amelia said with a smile. "When Anthony mentioned he had a housekeeper, I was afraid I wouldn't have anything to do, and yet here I am, choosing to do all my favorite chores."

Instead of asking Mrs. Hamilton where everything was, Amelia looked through the cabinets. It was nice to be able to find what she needed to do for her family.

She mixed enough dough for six loaves of bread, which was enough to feed all the children in the orphanage, and when she was done, she stared down at it. "I may be making too much," she said.

Mrs. Hamilton shook her head. "Not at all. As I said, I don't make bread often, and the boys and Mr. Martin love it. They'll have that much gone by tomorrow evening."

"And I can use the bread for toast in the morning. Maybe I'll make egg in a hole for everyone."

"What is egg in a hole?" Mrs. Hamilton asked.

Amelia smiled. "It's something the matron at the orphanage used to make for us when she was feeling like making a good breakfast. You take a piece of bread and cut out a hole in the middle of it. The matron always used a glass. And then you butter each side and put it in a skillet with butter. Then you cracked an egg into the hole, and you cooked it. Flip it once partway through, and you have egg in a hole."

Mrs. Hamilton smiled. "If you're making that, then I will be here in the morning for my egg in a hole."

"I'd love to cook an extra for you!"

Chapter Four

Amelia had just popped the bread into the oven when the boys ran into the house. She felt her heart leap at the boys' voices, and hurried out of the kitchen to join them. "Hello!"

Sam narrowed his eyes. "You don't look like a wicked stepmother."

Amelia grinned. "That's because I'm not wicked! I'm Amelia."

Sam walked over and offered his hand to shake. "We had a ma. We don't need a new one."

"That's all right. I'll just be your friend then. Did you know we're having brisket and potato salad and baked beans for supper?"

"It's not good without bread," Sam said, crossing his arms over his chest.

"Well, then it's a good thing I just put some rolls in the oven, isn't it?"

Ethan took a step toward her. "You made rolls?"

Amelia squatted so she would be on eye-level with Ethan. "I did! And you boys are going to have to sit at the table with me for a minute, and I want you to tell me all of your favorite foods, so I can make them for you."

Sam looked confused. "Mrs. Hamilton does all the cooking."

"She's going to let me cook sometimes too. I love to cook!"

Ethan's eyes grew wide. "You do?"

"I do! Let me get paper and a pencil." She looked around. "I don't know where it would live in your house. How can I make a list without paper and a pencil?"

Sam ran from the room, coming back with paper and a pencil. Amelia sat down at the table with the two objects. "I'll make a list for each of you, so I'll know what to make on your birthdays to make them super special."

The boys started telling her things to write down faster than she could write. When there was a lull, she asked, "Do you like chicken and dumplings?"

Sam shrugged. "We always get them at the diner."

"Then I'll put it on the list. It's my favorite thing in the whole wide world."

By the time they were finished with their list, Anthony came inside and stomped a few times to get the dirt off his boots. "What are you three up to?" he asked.

"The boys are telling me all their favorite foods, so I'll know what to make when I cook."

Anthony smiled. "I think you've already found one of their favorites. Bread."

"Doesn't it smell fabulous? I imagine that baking bread will be the scent that greets us in heaven."

Sam looked at his father. "She's not a wicked stepmother at all!"

Anthony laughed. "Why did you think she was?"

Ethan answered. "Ma used to tell us a story about a girl named Cinderella who had a wicked stepmother."

"So you thought all stepmothers were wicked?" Amelia asked, understanding their dilemma.

Both boys nodded. "Can we have a piece of bread before supper?" Ethan asked.

"I think supper's all ready!" Amelia said. She'd heard the back door open, and there was a male voice talking to Mrs. Hamilton. "Who wants to help me set the table?"

"We don't set the table," Sam said. "That's girls' work."

"All right," Amelia said, so happy to have the boys spending time with her. "I'll do it then!"

She set the table, setting five spots. "There's too many places," Sam said, frowning. "I can help you count."

"No, there's one for me," she held up one finger, "One for your pa," two fingers, "One for Mrs. Hamilton," three fingers, "One for each of you," five fingers. "I think I counted just right."

Sam looked at her. "Mrs. Hamilton doesn't eat with us."

"Well, I think she should!" Amelia said. "Do you two want to eat all alone?"

"No, ma'am," Ethan said, shaking his head and making his dark brown hair fly about his head.

"Then don't you think we should invite her to eat with us?" Amelia asked.

Sam looked at his father, who smiled and nodded. "Who's going to ask her?"

"We are!" Amelia said. "Come on boys!" She took their hands, and they went into the kitchen. "You'll eat with us, won't you?"

Mrs. Hamilton looked surprised. "I don't think that would be proper," she said.

"Why not? We're all one big happy family, aren't we?" Amelia asked.

"We want you to eat with us," Sam said.

"Please?" Ethan said.

Mrs. Hamilton smiled and nodded. "And your new ma told me what she's going to make for breakfast so I'm going to come over and eat breakfast in the morning."

The boys looked pleased and then tore away from Amelia to go to their father. "Mrs. Hamilton is going to eat with us because we're one big happy family!" Sam told him.

Anthony laughed. "That sounds very nice, doesn't it?"

"Yes. We love Mrs. Hamilton," Ethan said.

The two women put the food on the table together, including the huge platter of brisket and a big bowl full of dinner rolls. Ethan looked like he would do anything for one of the dinner rolls. "Wash your hands, boys," Amelia said.

The boys ran to the back of the house. "Why are they going back there?" she asked.

"You haven't spent much time looking around the house, have you?" Anthony asked.

"No..."

"The boys can reach the sink easier in the bathroom than they can in the kitchen, so they went there." Anthony walked into the kitchen and washed his own hands. "This all looks delicious. Whose idea was it to make rolls?"

"Amelia's," Mrs. Hamilton told him. "And she made loaves of bread for tomorrow as well."

"And the boys love her already," Anthony said, shaking his head. "How did you manage all that so quickly?"

Amelia shrugged. "I just know they're my children now, so I treated them like I would treat any child I loved."

Anthony was continually amazed by how kind his new wife was. He'd never met anyone quite like her.

They all sat down together as a family, though Mrs. Hamilton seemed like she felt out of place. "Let's hold hands as we pray," Amelia said.

All of them gripped each other's hands and Anthony thanked God for the food and for bringing Amelia safely all the way from Massachusetts. As soon as the prayer was over, both boys grabbed rolls, and Anthony surprised Amelia by grabbing three for himself.

They turned the brisket into little sandwiches, so Amelia followed suit. There hadn't been a lot of beef served at the orphanage, and she was glad to see how they ate it before making a fool of herself.

She complimented Mrs. Hamilton on everything on the table. "The potato salad is just dancing on my tastebuds!"

Sam narrowed his eyes. "Potatoes dance in your mouth? You have a strange mouth, Wicked Stepmother."

Amelia laughed. "You can just call me Amelia," she said.

"I like Wicked Stepmother," Sam said. "Especially now that I know you're not evil. May I call you that instead?"

"Absolutely. If it makes you smile, you can call me cow manure."

Both boys giggled while Anthony sat at the head of the table, shaking his head. He'd never seen a woman so good with children she didn't even know. "We were able to find all the missing calves," he said.

"Were only the calves missing?" Mrs. Hamilton asked. "That makes me feel like someone stole them."

Anthony nodded, sighing. "I wanted to believe that no one in this area would do such a thing, but it happened. I can't believe it was Mr. Lopez next door though. It had to be someone else. Perhaps someone who wanted me to think it was him."

"Maybe," Mrs. Hamilton said, but she looked unconvinced.

"Whoever it was, I'm going to have a cowboy on watch all night every night. One of them even volunteered. He said he likes it here when he's alone at night. I can't argue with that."

"Perhaps I could make a cake and take it to Mrs. Lopez and talk with her about what happened," Amelia said. "Surely it can't be the neighbor."

"I don't know what to say to that," Anthony said. "For now, stay home. You need to get to know the boys better and settle into your role here."

Amelia nodded. "I'll be making breakfast in the mornings so I won't miss cooking too terribly much," she said.

"I'm glad you enjoy cooking so much," Anthony said with a frown.

She shrugged. "I always have, and I'm sure I always will. Though I'm glad I'll have someone else who will cook as well," Amelia said. "Having a housekeeper is more than I ever dreamed possible. We'll split the work as best we can, but if one of us is sick, the other can take over easily."

By the time the meal was finished, Anthony realized that he really had gotten a good wife. Of all the orphans in the world, he'd gotten the one who would give you the shirt off her back if she thought it would be helpful.

She jumped up to help Mrs. Hamilton when it came time to do the dishes. "Do you want to wash or wipe?"

"I'll wipe," Mrs. Hamilton said. "It will be easier while you learn where everything goes."

Amelia nodded. "Sounds good to me."

The dishes took half an hour, and the women talked the entire time. "Thank you for inviting me to eat with the family," Mrs. Hamilton said. "In all my years here, I don't think anyone has ever even thought of that."

"Well, that's just plain silly. I'll expect you at the table for every meal, and I really will make you two eggs in holes tomorrow."

"It sounds delicious. I will eat them with a smile on my face." Mrs. Hamilton paused for a moment. "I'm glad you were the one to answer Mr. Martin's letter and come here. You're going to be very good for this family."

"I hope so. I want them to have the best lives they can." Amelia lowered her voice. "Ethan was much more talkative than I expected."

"I think that's because of the bread. You wouldn't believe how much those boys like bread, but my arthritis just doesn't let me make it very often anymore."

"I'm happy to be the bread maker in the family. What else can I take off your plate?" Amelia was already planning to do the laundry on Mondays, so Mrs. Hamilton didn't have to. She seemed much too old to be doing as much as she did.

Mrs. Hamilton shook her head. "That and you cleaning the upstairs will help me so much. I cannot believe how much you're willing to do."

"Well, they're my family, and I love them."

"You met them today!"

"But I've known of them for a month, and that's plenty long enough to fall in love with them, wouldn't you say?"

"I suppose that's true," Mrs. Hamilton said. "Thank you for being willing to work alongside me instead of just ordering me around."

"Of course! Anthony said you were his mother's friend, so you're part of the family, and you'll be treated as if you are!"

"Thank you," Mrs. Hamilton said, a tear in the corner of her eye. "I think you are just what Anthony and the boys need. Maybe they won't see it right away, but I do."

"Thank you! I can't think of anything you could have said to me that would make me happier."

"I'm so glad you're here."

Once the dishes were finished and the kitchen tidied up, Mrs. Hamilton walked to her house which really was only a short distance away. Amelia stood outside and watched her until she entered her home, worried that something could happen to her in that short distance.

When she went back inside, she joined Anthony and the boys in the parlor. Anthony was reading an almanac, and the boys were playing with blocks and wooden trains on the floor. "Dishes are done," she said as she joined the others.

Anthony looked up from his book, and the boys stopped what they were doing, all of them seeming to wait for her to entertain them. She was happy to do so.

"Texas sure is hotter than Massachusetts. I can't believe it's this hot in June. I don't want to think about how it will be in July and August."

Anthony sighed. "I'll tell you how it will be. Hot."

Amelia sat on the sofa beside Anthony. "How does everyone manage with the heat being so bad?"

He shrugged. "We sweat a lot. When I built this house, I made sure that I added as many windows as I could to help the breeze that will come through and cool us a bit. I tend to take a bath right before I go outside to start working, so I'll start out as cool as I can."

"And the boys?" she asked.

"They don't mind the heat as much as we adults do. When they get too hot, they go to the bathroom, fill a bucket of water, and dump it on their heads. That's Sam's favorite thing to do in the summer."

She laughed. "I'll help!"

Sam looked up at her. "Really?"

"Really! I may even dump a bucket of cold water on my head!" She couldn't believe how appealing the idea sounded.

"At least out here, we have a dry heat. Back in Fort Worth, it was so humid it felt as if we'd die in the same heat that isn't too terrible out here." Anthony shrugged. "Of course, there were more lakes, streams, and rivers there to jump into."

"That makes sense with it being a more humid area."

"Are you happy living here?"

Anthony nodded. "It's been harder since Mary died. She did most of the care for the boys, and I sometimes feel I don't know what to do with them."

"I can understand that," Amelia said. "Your whole life changed when she died, and so did the boys. It has to be harder without a mother. I wouldn't know because we only had matrons in the orphanage, and if one left, there was another right there to take her place, but that happened a few times. They would always have new rules, and the whole house would be confused for a bit, but we'd get used to it."

"How many children were in the orphanage?" he asked.

"Just twenty. There were always ten boys and ten girls. I was only a day or two old when I was left there, so I don't know of any other way of doing things. But I do know the rules I favored and the other children liked. So I think I can make up good rules for your family too."

Sam looked at her. "We don't like rules."

She laughed. "But you need them!"

"No, we don't." He turned back to the wall he was building, looking a bit put out. "Maybe you are a wicked stepmother after all."

Chapter Five

When it was bedtime for the boys, Amelia took them upstairs and helped them change into their sleep shirts. "Do you want me to tell you a story?" she asked. She'd always loved making up stories—especially for children.

Sam nodded. "But not Cinderella or Snow White. We know those stories. And we don't like Hansel and Grettel either!"

"Did your mama only tell you stories about wicked stepmothers?" Amelia asked, shaking her head. "There are so many other wonderful fairytales I could tell you, but tonight, I'm just going to tell a story that I made up. Is that all right?"

Both boys nodded happily.

Amelia cleared her throat dramatically and then began the story. "Once upon a time, in the heart of a magical forest, there was an adorable little bunny named Bella. Bella had fluffy white fur as soft as a cloud, and big, bright eyes that sparkled like stars. But what truly made Bella special was her heart—it was as warm and radiant as the sun itself.

"Bella loved to hop around the forest, making friends with everyone she met. From chatty sparrows to bashful hedgehogs, everyone in the forest adored Bella for her kindness and cheerful spirit.

"ONE WINTER, THE FOREST was enveloped in a thick blanket of snow. The trees wore coats of frost, and the air was filled with the crisp chill of winter. It was during this time that Bella met a lonely snowflake, named Solitary.

"Solitary was unique. Unlike other snowflakes that danced and twirled in the wind, Solitary quietly descended from the sky, feeling alone and out of place. When Bella saw Solitary, she saw a future friend in need." Looking at the boys, Amelia saw that Sam was mesmerized, but Ethan looked as if he was about to fall asleep.

"With a warm smile, Bella hopped over to Solitary. 'Why are you so quiet, dear snowflake?' she asked, her voice soft and soothing like a lullaby.

"'I don't fit in,' Solitary replied, its voice barely a whisper. 'I'm not like the other snowflakes.'

"Bella gave Solitary a comforting nuzzle. 'That's what makes you special, Solitary. You're not like any other snowflake because you're uniquely you. And that's beautiful.'

"Solitary blinked, surprised by Bella's words. No one had ever said anything like that to it before. A sense of warmth spread through Solitary, melting away its loneliness.

"From that day forward, Solitary wasn't lonely anymore. It found a friend in Bella, and learned that being different was something to be celebrated, not feared. And Bella found a unique friend in Solitary, adding to her collection of wonderful forest friends.

"As the winter passed and spring arrived, Solitary had to leave. But it promised to return next winter, and Bella waited patiently, knowing that when the first snow of winter fell, she would see her dear friend again.

"Remember that like Bella and Solitary, each of us is special in our own way. We should celebrate our uniqueness and be kind to one another.

"Now, it's time for you to close your eyes and drift into dreams. Dream of Bella, Solitary, and their magical forest adventures."

Sam had a big smile on his face. "I like your stories even better than I like the ones Ma told us."

"I'm glad. Goodnight, Sammy." She tucked the covers around him. "Goodnight, Ethan," she whispered as she did the same with the younger boy, who was already fast asleep. "I love you!"

She left the room and closed the door softly. It was nice that the boys shared a room. They would have each other for companionship if one got scared during the night.

After leaving the boys, she went into the room she would be sharing with Anthony, and dressed for sleep. She was very nervous about the night to come, but also very, very tired. Anthony wasn't there yet, so she climbed into bed and covered up, rolling to her side. She'd just close her eyes for a moment before Anthony came to bed.

When Amelia didn't return downstairs as he'd expected her to do, Anthony climbed the stairs to find Amelia sound asleep in bed. So much for their wedding night. He undressed and climbed into bed beside her, not wanting to wake her. She had to be exhausted after that long train ride.

It took him longer than usual to fall asleep himself, even though he was exhausted as well. He'd just been expecting the night to end very differently. Oh, well. There was always tomorrow night.

As was her habit, Amelia woke before the sun the following morning. When she saw Anthony asleep in bed beside her, she felt bad. Sure, she was happy for the reprieve and getting to know him for one more day before they consummated their marriage, but she felt badly for not giving him the wedding night he deserved. He'd made it clear that a big part of the reason he was marrying her was for marital comfort, but he'd let her sleep. In that moment, she knew she loved him.

She dressed quietly and went downstairs to start breakfast. After starting a fire in the stove, she cut off four slices of bread for Anthony, two for herself and Mrs. Hamilton, and one each for the boys. She buttered three sheet pans and put them into the oven to melt the butter, while she buttered all the slices of bread on just one side. Then she removed the sheet pans and put the piece of bread butter side up onto the pan, before taking a glass and cutting a perfect circle in each piece of bread before sliding all three pans back into the oven.

She found the basket of eggs on the counter, and she counted out ten eggs, finding the salt and pepper. Removing the sheet pans from the oven, she flipped each piece of bread, and put them back in for two more minutes.

After the two minutes were up, she removed the perfectly round circle from each of the pieces of bread set them onto a clean plate for everyone to use to dip into the egg yolk. Then she broke an egg into each of the holes, being sure to salt and pepper each of them.

Looking out the window, she could see Mrs. Hamilton coming toward the house, so she stuck the first sheet pan full of her concoction into the oven.

When Mrs. Hamilton stepped inside, she said, "Oh, that smells wonderful!"

"No one else is up yet, so I'm just making ours. It'll be ready in a couple of minutes."

"Have you put the coffee on yet?" Mrs. Hamilton asked.

"Oh, I didn't think to!"

"I'll do it. Mr. Martin and I are fond of our coffee in the mornings." Mrs. Hamilton immediately got out the coffee pot and started the coffee.

When Amelia removed the eggs from the oven, she popped two onto each of two plates before adding two toast circles to each as well. "Shall we have our breakfast?" she asked. "I'll start the rest of the eggs when our men come down."

Amelia sat with Mrs. Hamilton eating her breakfast with a glass of milk from the ice box. As soon as the coffee was ready, Mrs. Hamilton got herself a cup, and Amelia heard footsteps on the stairs.

Looking up and seeing Anthony, Amelia got up and put his eggs into the oven, pouring him a cup of coffee. "The eggs need a few minutes," she told him as she came out of the kitchen and saw him sitting at the table. "I didn't know when you'd be up, and I was afraid they'd get cold." She put his coffee on the table in front of him.

"Happy to have the coffee," he said, taking a sip. He looked curiously at the food she still had left on her plate. "What is that?"

"I call them eggs in a hole. The matron found the receipt in the Boston cookbook, but they were called eggs in a hat. They look more like they're in a hole to me, though, so that's what I call them."

She picked up her toast circle and dipped it into the yolk of her second egg and ate the bite. He smiled, looking at it curiously. "That really does look good."

Amelia got up and went back into the kitchen to check on his eggs. When she saw they were done, she put them onto a plate, adding four of the toast circles. Putting them in front of Anthony, she smiled. "I do hope you'll enjoy them as much as I do." She sat back down and continued eating her eggs, looking at Mrs. Hamilton. "What do you think?"

Mrs. Hamilton nodded. "They're delicious. I think I'd like this any time of day."

Anthony nodded. "I agree. And the boys will love them!"

"I have one each for the boys ready to pop into the oven as soon as they make an appearance." Amelia finished up her own eggs, but decided not to get up again, instead enjoying the company of her husband and housekeeper.

"The only way they'd be better is if we had bacon to go with them," Anthony said. "I do love bacon."

Amelia nodded. "I didn't think of that. At the orphanage, we felt blessed to have eggs or bacon with our breakfast. I don't remember ever having both."

Anthony looked at his wife for a moment, wondering how she was so happy all the time with what sounded to him like a terrible childhood. "Maybe next time then."

"Of course!" she said. "What do you like to have for breakfast?"

He shrugged. "Mrs. Hamilton usually makes scrambled eggs with toast and bacon."

"But you like having eggs other ways?" she asked. She could remember some breakfasts at the orphanage that she had loved, but they were always special meals that they had very seldom.

"Yes, of course!"

"Maybe tomorrow, I'll do eggs, bacon, and fried potatoes. I love to mix my egg yolk through my fried potatoes, and eat them that way."

"That sounds wonderful," he said.

Mrs. Hamilton nodded. "Expect me for breakfast tomorrow as well."

"Do you like pancakes and johnny cakes?" Amelia asked.

He nodded. "I'm easy to feed. If there are meat and potatoes, with a meal, I'm happy."

"I'm sorry I didn't think to serve either with breakfast this morning!" Amelia said. "Tomorrow I'll serve both, and that should make up for it."

When the boys came down, she put their eggs in the oven as they were using the bathroom. By the time they sat down at the table, their food was ready. As they looked down at the eggs, Sam looked confused. "Like this," Anthony said, dipping his circle into the yolk and eating it.

The boys both tried it, looking happy. "Delicious!" Sam said, taking another bite.

Little Ethan followed suit, and though he didn't say anything, his whole face lit up as he ate his egg, and it was gone quickly. "Do you boys need more? Perhaps I should have made three for you to share." Amelia looked at them worriedly.

Ethan rubbed his tummy. "I'm too full."

Sam nodded his agreement.

"All right," Amelia said standing up. "Just let me clear the table, and we can go for a walk when the dishes are done. All right, boys?"

They both nodded.

In the kitchen, she fixed a sink full of soapy water and saw that Mrs. Hamilton was right there to dry the dishes. "Where will you go on your walk?" Mrs. Hamilton asked.

"I thought we'd walk up the road a bit. See what we see."

"If you are so inclined, the blackberries and blueberries in the garden look ripe. It might be better to work on that this morning than going for a walk."

"Oh, that would be a fun project with the boys! And I can make jam and pie filling to put up for the winter."

Mrs. Hamilton smiled. "You couldn't be more different than the first Mrs. Martin."

"I don't know if that's good or bad, but I'm going to take that as a compliment as I refuse to believe you would insult me."

"It's definitely a compliment," Mrs. Hamilton said. "I'm afraid Mary would spend all summer indoors with cold cloths on her face. If any gardening was to be done, I was the one doing it."

"Oh, well that's certainly not right." Amelia shook her head. "If my family will be eating it, then I will be growing it."

"I planted the blackberry bushes when she was expecting Sam, and I probably planted a few too many. I can never get them all harvested."

"The boys and I will help with that," Amelia said, smiling. "Where would I find buckets to put the ripe berries in?"

As soon as the breakfast dishes were done, Amelia found three tin pails, giving one to each of the boys, and keeping one for herself. "We're not going to take a walk," she told them, excitement in her voice. "We're going to pick blackberries and blueberries, and then I'm going to make a blackberry pie for dessert tonight."

The boys looked genuinely excited at the change in plans. They went outside, and she showed them how to tell if a blackberry was ripe. "Now, I want to see more berries in the buckets than in your mouths, all right?"

The boys went through first, picking the berries, and she noticed many going into mouths instead of into the pails, but that was to be expected with two small boys. She found the ones they missed, putting them into her bucket. She only let herself try one berry. She so preferred blackberries to be in pie or jam.

They spent the entire morning picking berries, which meant she picked berries all morning, and the boys helped for a while before ending up building things in the dirt on the edges of the garden. She didn't mind though. She was used to that sort of behavior from the younger children of the orphanage.

When all three buckets were full, she told the boys they were going inside. She was surprised at the sheer amount of berries, but she could already taste that pie for supper. Hopefully, Mrs. Hamilton wouldn't mind if she took over the kitchen that afternoon, making pie filling. She'd wait for the next afternoon to make the jam.

And she had yet to pick the blueberries. She'd never seen so many berries in her life. The orphanage had kept them fed, but treats were few and far between. Oh, how she loved her new family, and Texas.

Chapter Six

Mrs. Hamilton was quite happy to let Amelia rustle around in her kitchen and make pie filling that afternoon. Trying to think ahead, Amelia made a huge batch of pie filling, using all three pails of blackberries. She'd still have plenty of blackberries after a day of cooking though. She felt like they'd barely scratched the surface, and it was glorious to see there wouldn't be a shortage of sweets. Amelia had never known such wealth!

While she cooked, Mrs. Hamilton cleaned. The boys were tucked away in their beds for their naps, and Amelia took the opportunity to roll out a crust for the pie.

When Mrs. Hamilton returned to the kitchen, Amelia asked about canning supplies. "Oh, of course! I'll run and get them for you."

When Mrs. Hamilton came back with the supplies, she immediately washed them and got them ready to use while Amelia stirred her pie filling. She dipped a spoon into her mixture and tasted a quick bite after blowing on it vigorously. There was no burn like hot fruit burn. "Oh, that's perfect. And we'll be able to have it throughout the winter. I'll put enough for one pie into each jar."

"We'll put enough for one pie into each jar," Mrs. Hamilton corrected. "I'm starting to worry you're going to do all my work, and I won't have a way to make a living!"

Amelia laughed. "It won't happen. I enjoy having you here too much. We work well together, and there will be times I'll need a lot of help." Amelia started spooning the pie filling into the clean jars.

"You have no idea how much you're going to be appreciated in this house."

"I already love it here," Amelia said. "What are you making for supper?" She'd noticed some steaks that look to have been pounded to within an inch of their lives on the counter.

"Chicken fried steak, mashed potatoes, and green beans. I figure we'll do a blackberry pie for dessert!"

"Oh, yes we will! There's a lot in that garden that's already ready to be harvested. I noticed that a lot of strawberries died right on the vine. I wish you'd had help before I got here."

"The boys picked enough for us to have a strawberry shortcake, and they filled their tummies a few times."

"Then I suppose it's not all a huge waste. Next year they'll be put to good use."

Soon the jars were filled, and Mrs. Hamilton said she'd finish the canning process. "I can't let you do all the work!"

Amelia laughed. "I'm going to put on my bonnet and get some blueberries then. All of the blackberries aren't quite ripe, but they will be by the end of the week. I sure would like to have lots of both set aside for winter."

"Did you learn to garden and can at the orphanage?"

"Oh, yes. It was part of what was expected of the girls. The boys did the weeding and occasionally, they would hunt for meat for our suppers, but mostly, they made sure the yard was kept up and the food was eaten."

"That sounds like boys."

Amelia took the three pails and hurried upstairs to get her bonnet. She hadn't worn one that morning, and her face felt plenty hot now.

As she went through the blueberries, she was again surprised at the sheer number of them she found. It saddened her how the garden had been neglected, and she knew that she and the boys had their work cut out for them.

She filled only one pail before Anthony came home for the day. "Are you early? Or am I taking too much time?" she asked.

"I'm a little earlier than usual. I like to stop early on Saturdays to spend what's left of the day with the boys." He looked her up and down, finding the sight of her wearing a pretty blue dress, and a white bonnet very appealing. She even wore an apron to cover her entire dress. As far as he knew, Mary hadn't owned an apron. "What are you doing?"

"Harvesting blueberries. Mrs. Hamilton is finishing up the blackberry pie filling I made from the blackberries the boys and I picked this morning." She shook her head. "I hope you like blackberry pie because we're having it for dessert along with what she called chicken fried steak, which I've never even heard of."

He grinned. "It's a dish that was created here in Texas on one of the cattle drives. As the cows walk, they get leaner and leaner, so they have more muscle, and the meat isn't as tender. So one of the cooks on the trail took some of the steak that had too many muscles and pounded it to make it more tender, and then dipped it in an egg wash and flour, frying it as if it was a chicken. Hence the name chicken fried steak. It's a well-loved meat around here."

"It sounds good to me. I've seen steak before, but I've never had the opportunity to try it. I'm sure I'll love it!" She had enjoyed the small amount of beef she'd eaten. Usually when there had been meat for supper at the orphanage, it was chicken. They'd raised chickens and when they had a rooster, it almost always went into the pot.

"You can't live on a ranch and say you've never eaten steak!" Anthony shook his head. "I'll ask Mrs. Hamilton to serve steak one day next week. You'll see how good it is."

"The brisket last night was very tasty. I'm sure I'll love steak!"

She kept picking berries while they talked. "I'm going to get a bath before supper," he said. "Then when the boys wake up from their nap, I'll be ready to play with them. You should probably stop soon. Your face is getting bright red."

"I forgot to wear my bonnet this morning. I'll do better next time."

She carried the bucket of blueberries in as soon as it was full. Mrs. Hamilton had potatoes on to boil, and she was frying up the steaks. "I'm going to make blueberry muffins to go with our breakfast tomorrow," Amelia told the older woman. "Next time I want to watch you make the chicken fried steak. I'd never even heard of it, but from the way Anthony described it, I think I'll need to know how to make it on occasion."

Mrs. Hamilton laughed. "Some men eat it for breakfast as well. It's a very popular dish here in Texas."

"I can see that. I even got a little history lesson on where chicken fried steak came from." The jars of blackberry pie filling were all spread out on the counter on towels. "I need to remember to label those tonight before bed."

"I'll do it in the morning," Mrs. Hamilton said. "You're doing too much work. You need to pace yourself."

Amelia shook her head. "Remember what I told you. Me being idle is never a good thing."

Amelia noticed her pie was already in the oven, and she got plates down to set the table. It was nice to be able to work with another woman. She was used to having all her friends around her as she cooked and cleaned. It was what made the orphanage such a wonderful place to live.

She saw the boys come downstairs, and they hurried to the parlor where she heard Anthony's greeting. "I heard you two helped your new ma harvest the blackberries this morning!"

"Now we get pie!" Amelia wasn't sure which boy said that, but she thought it was Ethan. He sounded very excited about pie.

She popped her head into the kitchen. "How much longer for supper?" She wasn't overly hungry, but she knew her men all had an appetite.

"About thirty minutes. I need to finish frying up the steaks, mash the potatoes, and get the pie out of the oven and cooling."

"Wonderful. And you'll eat with us again," Amelia said. Now that she'd asked once, she planned to include Mrs. Hamilton in every meal.

Mrs. Hamilton smiled and nodded. "I would love to eat with the family again."

There were still some of the dinner rolls from the night before, but Amelia knew she'd need to have bread dough mixed up before church the following morning. "How far is the church from here?" she asked.

"It's a ten-minute drive. It's in the same building as the school."

"And do you know what time service is?" Amelia asked.

"Starts at ten."

"Oh, good. That gives me plenty of time to do things in the morning."

Mrs. Hamilton smiled. "I think so too."

When they sat down for their meal, Amelia was surprised that everyone put gravy on their chicken fried steak. "You didn't tell me about the gravy!" Amelia said, ready to lick her lips in excitement. There hadn't often been extra flour lying around for gravy at the orphanage. She loved gravy.

As she took her first bite, she smiled. "I like this!"

Mrs. Hamilton nodded and smiled. "It's one of my favorites."

Anthony looked at the older woman. "My wife told me today that she's never eaten steak. Would you be willing to make steak for us next week?"

"Yes, of course. I'll make anything you ask for. You know that."

"Except bread," Ethan said, as he popped a big piece of a dinner roll into his mouth.

"That's because I won't let her make bread because I like doing it so much," Amelia said.

Ethan shook his head as he popped more bread into his mouth.

Sam methodically forked the pieces of chicken fried steak into his mouth, barely taking a break to breathe. "I guess you like chicken fried steak, Sam," Amelia said.

Sam chewed all of the food in his mouth, which took a good long while with the way he'd been packing it in. Finally, he said, "It's my favorite."

"I think it might be my favorite too," Amelia said as she took another bite of the gravy-covered meat. "Next time I'm going to have Mrs. Hamilton teach me to make it."

Ethan frowned. "You know how to make bread, but not chicken fried steak?"

Amelia nodded. "Someone didn't teach me the most important things."

After the dishes were done that night, and Amelia had watched Mrs. Hamilton walk to her own home, she joined the family in the parlor.

This time, Anthony wasn't reading, and his boys had his full attention. "It was fun picking berries, but we played in the dirt too," Sam said.

Ethan nodded. "But our wicked stepmother picked so many berries!"

Amelia grinned. "We forgot to have pie," she said, shaking her head. "I guess I'll have to feed it to the chickens."

"No!" Ethan said, his voice a wail.

"Should we all go back to the table, and I'll serve pie?"

Both boys seemed very excited. "Only if you promise me one thing..." Anthony said.

"What's that?" Amelia asked.

"You can't do the dishes tonight. They have to wait until morning."

She frowned at him. "We'll get bugs! And do you know how hard it is to wash plates after they've had blackberry pie filling caked onto them?"

He narrowed his eyes. "You can wash them, but leave them on a towel on the counter to drip dry."

She sighed. It didn't feel right leaving work to be done overnight. "All right. I can do that." It wouldn't be easy, but she could do it.

She put a fork and a small plate at each of their seats, and then cut up the pie, serving it for them all. When she took her first bite, she smiled. It had turned out perfectly. She was a better cook than she'd realized.

After washing the small plates and forks, she put a plate over what was left of the pie. "Are you boys ready for bed?" she asked.

Ethan nodded. "Will you tell us a story again?"

Amelia laughed at the question. "I sure will."

As she climbed the stairs with the boys, Anthony called out, "Come down when the boys are in bed."

Amelia smiled at her husband and nodded, not sure how she had been so incredibly fortunate to end up married to a man she already loved and had two wonderful little boys. She even liked it when they called her their wicked stepmother.

Fifteen minutes later, after their story, Amelia went back downstairs and joined her husband in the parlor. "The best part of having children is when they go to bed, and we have some private time," Anthony told her as she sat beside him on the sofa.

"I'm sorry I fell asleep last night," she told him. "I just meant to close my eyes until you joined me, but I was so tired. I didn't sleep well on the train. I hope you can forgive me."

"Of course," he said, stroking her cheek with the back of one finger. "I would like to have that wedding night tonight, though."

She blushed but nodded. "Of course. It's part of the reason I'm here."

"You know, I wasn't terribly worried about whether I would find a wife who was willing to cook, clean, and work in the garden. But now that you're here and doing those things, I am so happy to see you willing to work for the family."

"I just can't sit idle," Amelia said. "My hands are supposed to always be working on something. I'd love to find all your mending that piled up and go to work on it in the evenings."

"You don't always have to be working," he told her.

She shrugged. "I feel like I should."

"Every once in a while, it's good to have fun and to enjoy one another." He stared deeply into her eyes. "I haven't even really kissed you yet. I didn't want our first kiss to be in front of the pastor and his wife."

She smiled. "I didn't either. I've never been kissed, so it was something I was hoping to enjoy in private. No one needs to watch."

He grinned, tilting her chin up with one finger. When his lips lowered to hers, she let out a gasp of surprise. It was no wonder they weren't allowed to kiss in the orphanage. It felt much too good for everyone to just be running around doing it with anyone they chose.

She put her arms around his shoulders and held on to him, hoping the kiss would last forever.

When he broke off the kiss, he stood and took her hand. "I think it's time for us to go to bed."

She nodded, ready to follow him to the ends of the earth.

Chapter Seven

Amelia's heart felt as if it was pounding out of her chest as she stepped into the bedroom and Anthony closed the door. As usual, when she was nervous, she started talking. "So am I supposed to put my nightgown on with you in the room? Or should I wait for you to go and put it on? What's the right way to do—"

His mouth closed over hers again, cutting off her words. While they kissed, she felt his hands all over her, and then she realized he was unbuttoning the front of her dress. Was he going to put her nightgown on for her? Oh, she wished she knew what she was supposed to be doing.

When his hand slipped inside her dress, and cupped her breast through her petticoat, she forgot all about what she'd been thinking and simply kissed him back. Her fingers went to the front of his shirt, and she began liberating the buttons from their holes. She didn't know or care if it was the right thing to do. She wanted to feel his bare flesh against hers.

Just as she pushed his shirt off his shoulders, she felt him push her dress down. Standing before him in just her petticoat felt nice. She'd never taken to wearing a corset because she was naturally slender, and the orphanage hadn't been willing to pay for one. When they'd been donated, they'd gone to the girls who needed them more than she did.

She felt her petticoat being unbuttoned and broke free. "My nightgown is on the dresser."

He shook his head. "You don't need it tonight. It's too hot for a nightgown."

She couldn't argue with that, but she felt funny standing before him in nothing but her knickers. And then the knickers were gone, and it was just her, standing naked in front of her husband, the man she loved.

"Are you sure? Is it all right for you to see me naked? I can put it on—"

His kiss stopped her. She was starting to get the impression he didn't think she should talk so much as they kissed.

He lifted her into his arms and put her gently onto the bed. When she looked at him, he was still wearing his denim pants, and she had to wonder how that was going to work. "Don't you need to take your pants off for this to work? Or am I confused about what we're going to do?" The matron hadn't been very descriptive when she'd told her what would happen between her and her husband.

Anthony laughed. "I know what to do, and I'll take care of you."

She propped herself up on her elbows, half-sitting on the bed. "But don't you think it would be—"

His finger covered her lips. "You have two choices. You can watch me take my pants off, or you can close your eyes."

She considered for a moment, and though she knew it was not very ladylike of her, she wanted to watch. She'd changed lots of baby boys, of course, but she'd never seen a man without his pants.

So she kept her eyes on that portion of him as she dropped his pants and drawers to the floor. What sprang out of his drawers surprised her. She'd thought they were all tiny little things, and his…well, it wasn't.

Before she could comment on his body, he climbed into the bed with her, his mouth coming down directly on hers. It was almost as if he was afraid of what she'd say next.

As he kissed her, his hands roamed over her body, trying to bring her to the same level of need he was at. He didn't want to hurt her and he was afraid he would after all the months without a woman.

When one hand moved between her thighs and touched her in a place she'd never been touched, she gasped, arching off the bed and into his hand. That was good enough for him. He rolled atop her and settled between her spread thighs. "This may hurt a little."

"Of course, it's going to hurt! That thing of yours is not tiny like the baby boys I've—" She finished her sentence against his lips and a moment later, she felt the thing that was a part of him slide inside her.

It did hurt a little, but he held still until she moved, wondering how long he would stay inside her that way. Surely she was already pregnant, and their time together was over.

And then he began to move inside her, in and out, and she clung to his shoulders, surprised at how very good it felt. The matron hadn't said it would feel good. She was sure it wasn't supposed to. Was she a wanton woman?

He kept kissing her, and she stayed quiet as he moved inside her, and finally, she felt something there that surprised her, and she squeezed him even tighter.

He moved a few more times, and then he moved into her and stopped. As he lay there, still on top of her, he buried his face into her neck.

Slowly he rolled to his back. "I needed that."

"What happens when you don't get it?" she asked, wondering how he'd survived for so long between wives if he needed it so badly.

He opened one eye and peered at her. "I'd probably die."

"Well, I don't want you to die, but now that there's a baby in me, can we do it again?" She promised herself she would never say no to having relations with her husband. As much as she'd enjoyed the first time, she was certain she'd always enjoy it.

"You won't get pregnant every time," he said softly. This wasn't the time and place to give her a lesson on how her body worked, but she seemed to know virtually nothing.

"I won't?" She frowned. That wasn't what Matron had led her to believe. "Is it all right that it felt good?"

He grinned, rolling to his side and facing her. "Yes, it's perfectly fine. God made it for man and woman to enjoy one another within a marriage."

"Oh good. I really liked it at the end. When can we do it again?"

"Men need a little time to recover, but morning would work. Or if one of us wakes up during the night..."

"Well, I already liked being married, but I think this new aspect of things is going to make me love it even more. I thought it was too big, but I must be stretchier than I realized."

He couldn't help but laugh. "You make me happy, Amelia."

"Oh, good, because you make me happy as well." Her eyes traveled down his body to see that he was much smaller than he had been. "It's shrunk!"

"It will grow again. I promise."

"Oh good. I don't want to be done with that." She blinked a few times. "I'm sleepy now. Is that good?"

"I would think so, since it's bedtime. What do you have planned for tomorrow?" he asked, softly stroking her shoulder. Her skin was so soft, he liked touching it.

"More berry picking. I'll make blueberry pie filling, and then I'll start jam. There are so many berries!" She smiled at him. "I hope you have a sweet tooth."

"Oh, trust me, I do."

She turned to her side to sleep and was pleasantly surprised when he wrapped an arm around her and fitted himself to her back. She felt loved and protected as she fell asleep, held close in his arms.

She was still in his arms when she woke in the morning, and she had to carefully extricate herself from his embrace. She dressed in the dark and waited until she was downstairs to put her shoes on.

After starting a fire in the stove, she quickly peeled and cut up potatoes. She liked to boil them before she fried them for a better-tasting breakfast potato, and then she put a sheet pan filled with bacon into the oven. She had a hard time cooking bacon without splashing herself with grease, and she found it much easier to cook in the oven all at once.

As soon as the potatoes were finished, she fished them out with a slotted spoon and added them to an already-greased frying pan. When everyone started down the stairs, she'd start their eggs, but she wanted everything else ready for now.

She sliced off a few pieces of the bread they had left and toasted it in the oven. She stood over the stove, stirring the potatoes to keep them from burning. When they were finished, she put them into a bowl beside the stove, wondering when the family would join her.

She heard footsteps on the stairs, and when Anthony came into view, she asked how he wanted his eggs, then hurried into the kitchen to fix them for him. Pulling the bacon from the oven, she added bacon and some of the potatoes to his plate before taking up his eggs and putting them on the plate as well.

"Were the boys stirring yet?" she asked as she put the plate on the table in front of him.

He nodded. "They both like their eggs the same way I do," he said, watching as she hurried back into the kitchen to start an egg for each boy.

She dropped her eggs into the same pan, thinking she could get up to cook Mrs. Hamilton's eggs or she could fix her own. Amelia would be happy either way. It felt good to do for the older woman who was always taking care of everyone else.

She just sat down with the boys and her plate when Mrs. Hamilton came in. "How do you want your eggs?" Amelia asked.

"I'll make my own eggs," Mrs. Hamilton said. "There's no need for you to get up."

Amelia had put a pile of buttered toast in the middle of the table, and everyone grabbed what they wanted. Amelia enjoyed her breakfast immensely. "This bacon is so good!"

Anthony smiled. "There's a hog farmer up the street. I trade him beef for bacon and ham. It all works out for us both."

"Well, the next time you see him, tell him how very good his bacon is."

"He'll be at church this morning."

"Mrs. Hamilton said church starts at ten. Could you get the boys into the tub this morning while I mix up dough for bread? That way it can rise while we're at church."

Anthony nodded. "I'm happy to help."

"Oh, good. I want to pick more berries today as well."

He shook his head. "No. I want you to spend the day with the boys and me. You can pick berries tomorrow."

She bit her lip. "I really can't sit idle. What do you want to do?"

"Let's go for a drive. Mrs. Hamilton, would you mind if we had supper in town this evening? The diner in town has steak, and I think my wife has lived longer than anyone should without trying it."

Mrs. Hamilton nodded. "I'll even bake the bread and make jam from the blueberries while you're gone."

"Oh, that sounds delicious," Amelia said. "But I don't want to leave you here to do all the work yourself."

Anthony shook his head. "You know she works here, and you're my wife, right?"

"I have somehow figured that out along the way," Amelia said. She fretted about what to do while they were driving. She knew it would be a full hour there and an hour back. "I'll take my knitting along!"

He frowned. "Why?"

"To keep my hands busy. I'm sure the children need new socks anyway."

He shook his head. "You really won't sit idle?"

"I can't. Something happens in my brain and it wants to explode when I don't do anything. It's my job to always stay busy." She tilted her head to one side. "Maybe that's why Matron liked me so much. I was always looking for more chores."

He sighed. "We need to teach you to relax. Don't you ever just sit down with a good book?"

She shrugged. "For an hour or two, but then I need to get up and move around. And have you seen the garden? There's so much to do!"

"We're going to town. Take your knitting if you have to."

After the breakfast dishes were done, Amelia mixed up the dough for the bread, kneading it on the counter. "I hate leaving you alone all day," she whispered to Mrs. Hamilton.

"I like having days to myself from time to time. I wouldn't like it all the time, but I'll be fine for today."

"Oh, good. I don't want you to feel left out."

"I don't."

She took her turn in the bathtub a short while later, washing her hair and brushing it dry. She put on her new white dress that she had yet to wear. "I was going to wear this for our wedding," she told Anthony when he complimented her on it. "But you were in a hurry, so I didn't even ask to change."

"It's beautiful, and so is the woman inside it," he said, leaning down to kiss her softly.

"I sure did enjoy our time last night," she whispered.

He nodded. "I did too. We'll have to make a habit of doing that."

"Oh, good. That sounds like a lovely activity."

At church, he introduced her to the other ladies who were there. Only about ten families attended the church instead of going all the way into Midland, but they seemed like a good mix to her.

The boys had friends they played with after the service, and she found the other women very friendly and kind. "Mary was my closest friend," one woman said. "I know Anthony and the boys will always miss her."

Amelia nodded. "They do miss her a great deal."

Just then, Ethan came and tugged on her dress. "Wicked Stepmother?"

Amelia smiled at him. "Do you need something?"

"I fell down." Tears popped into his eyes as he told her.

She squatted down and wiped away his tears, kissing his cheek. "There. Do you feel better?"

Ethan nodded and ran back to his friends.

The woman she'd been talking to, who had introduced herself as Alice frowned at Amelia. "The boys call you wicked stepmother?"

Amelia nodded, grinning. "Apparently their mother told them the stories of Cinderella, Snow White, and Hansel and Gretel, all of whom had wicked stepmothers. So, they call me Wicked Stepmother. It makes me smile."

Alice frowned. "I wouldn't take that with a smile. I would ask them to call you Ma or Amelia."

"I really think it's cute. They can call me whatever they want as long as they come to me when they're hurt or upset. Why would it matter?"

The other woman gave her an odd look as she moved on to talk to someone else. Amelia didn't mind though. She hadn't found Alice to be overly nice anyway.

Chapter Eight

As they drove toward town, Amelia mentioned how Alice had reacted to the boys calling her Wicked Stepmother. "I think it's funny, and I love it, but she seemed to think it was wrong that I even let them call me that."

Anthony shook his head. "I think you would have let the boys call you anything they came up with, and you'd have liked it. Alice is...well, she's more like Mary was. Everything has to be perfect in every way, but she's not willing to lift a finger to make it perfect." He shook his head. "I don't know how I thought that was acceptable behavior for a wife."

"Because you loved her!" Amelia said. "Sometimes, you see people through rose-colored glasses, and you only see what's good about them, and I think that's a wonderful thing. It means you care about them deeply. You see me for who I truly am because you had no feelings for me when we married. You'll love me soon, but I can wait."

Anthony blinked a few times. Only Amelia would tell him he would love her soon. She was special, but he wasn't certain if she was special in a good, healthy way. Oh, she lifted his spirits more than anyone else could, but if a man tried to break into their house and hurt her, would she offer to cook him a meal so he'd have more strength for his plans?

"That may be it," he said.

The boys were both in the back of the wagon, and Amelia turned to see if they were all right. Both were lying down in the wagon, and they were talking softly to one another.

"The boys look content. Do you make this trip with them often?"

He shrugged. "We made it more often before their mother died. She wanted to be able to be around more people than our little country church can accommodate, so she'd beg me to take her to church in town. We went to our country church every other week, and then to the church in Midland every other week. It's not a large city by any means, but it's a prominent cattle shipping center, so there are often people around who aren't from here. She never seemed to mind who was there, as long as there were people."

"I like people as well, but I'm plenty happy in your small country church." She wasn't worried that Alice didn't seem to like her. What difference did that make? She was still a future friend, but it would just take her a little longer to convince her to be that friend. "Tell me about this diner we're going to."

He shrugged. "It's open seven days a week because the train runs seven days a week. We came here after church most weeks that we came to the church here. They serve a variety of things, and it's mostly people from the train who come here. They'll have an hour or two to pass, and this is a good place to do it."

"And you always get the steak?" she asked.

"Always. They serve a lot of different things, but steak is a favorite of mine. I think you'll enjoy it as well."

"I'm certain I will," she said. "I'm really looking forward to trying it."

"Is there anything you don't look forward to?" he asked.

She thought about it for a moment. "I don't look forward to the pain of childbirth," she said, "but I look forward to the baby I'll have when it's all over."

He grinned, thinking about her being so sure she was expecting the night before after they'd made love. She was innocent and sweet. He knew she was the right new mother for the boys, even if she did teach them that everything is perfect all the time.

As they drove, she asked about different people she'd met at church that morning. "It was a lovely service. I didn't get a chance to meet the pastor's wife, though."

"We have a young, unmarried pastor," Anthony said. "When he first came, I think every unmarried lady in the congregation over the age of thirteen set her cap for him. He's been here three years now, and I haven't seen him so much as court one of them."

"I didn't know pastors could be unmarried!" Amelia shook her head. "I mean, every pastor I've ever had has been older, married, with children. And you have a pastor who is a bachelor. Very unusual."

He nodded. "Our last pastor retired and he and his wife moved to live near his son and grandchildren. When we got this new pastor, several of us men were unhappy about it because it just didn't seem right to have one so young. But we all like him, and his sermons are always about something we need to think about."

"I did like his sermon this morning. I love it when a preacher takes on the topic of loving your neighbor and exactly what that should mean for all of us."

He nodded. "I agree. Sometimes I feel guilty about what I hear, but I do think it's an important message for the whole congregation. I think the pastor could preach on it every week, and it would never be enough."

He stopped the wagon beside a small diner, moving it off the main street. The boys scrambled down, but she remembered to wait for him to help her to the ground. She still wasn't certain why women were treated as if they could do nothing by themselves, but she didn't mind too much.

As they walked into the diner, she noticed that they were the only people there other than the staff. Anthony held her chair for her, and since no man had ever done that before, she wasn't certain when she should plop her backside onto the chair.

Finally, they got it right, and the boys just watched her. "What are you going to eat, Wicked Stepmother?" Sam asked.

"Your pa thinks I should try a steak. I've never had one."

Sam shrugged. "I like steak, but I like chicken and dumplings better!"

"Oh, they have chicken and dumplings?" It was a favorite meal of Amelia's, but she could easily make it for supper one night. "What are you going to eat, Ethan?"

"Chicken and dumplings," Ethan said.

Amelia looked at Anthony. "Mrs. Hamilton never makes chicken and dumplings, so the boys get it every time we come here."

"I'll have to make it one day soon," she said, smiling. "At least I'll know I won't be the only one enjoying it."

A tired-looking woman came to the table then. "Do you know what you want?"

Anthony ordered for all four of them, and she wandered off. "She looks so tired," Amelia said. "Should I offer to cook it and bring it to the table?"

He shook his head. "No, one of the best things about eating out is you don't have to cook, serve, or do the dishes."

"But I don't feel as tired as she looks," Amelia protested.

"Just enjoy the experience."

Amelia wasn't sure how to enjoy it. Her hands were idle. She could hear Matron softly whisper, "Idle hands are the devil's workshop."

She shook her head. "I'm afraid I don't know how to enjoy sitting still with nothing to do. Is that even possible?"

He couldn't help but compare her in his mind to Mary. Here she was wishing for something to do with her hands, while his first wife would sit there, unmoving for hours at a time. She believed that Mrs. Hamilton should do everything, and she should do nothing.

"Were you not allowed to sit after your chores were done at the orphanage?" he asked.

"Yes. But I would finish my chores and then ask the others if I could do their chores so I wouldn't just be sitting there, and everyone was happy for me to do their chores, so it was very rare I sat. It got harder later because Matron would notice me doing others' work, and tell them they had to do their own. So I would find some of the old donated clothes that were too filled with holes to actually work for one of us to wear, and I'd make a quilt out of it for one of the babies. We got new babies all the time, though they were adopted out easily."

"No one ever talked about adopting you?" he asked.

"Oh, sure! I had two different families take me home with them, but they brought me back."

He frowned. "Why did they take you back?"

"The first time, the wife found me up scrubbing the floors in the middle of the night, and she thought that was strange, and she didn't want a child who was awake when she wasn't, so she took me back the next day. I was more careful with the second family so I stayed in bed all night, but I spent all my time in the kitchen, helping the housekeeper, and they didn't want that, so they took me back too." She shrugged. "I always preferred to be at the orphanage anyway. There, no one complained if I did extra. Well, only Matron when I did the others' chores."

He shook his head. "Have you never been able to sit still?"

"No. When I was a baby, the doctor thought the matron must not be feeding me because I couldn't gain weight, but then he watched me for a moment, and I was flipping all over the place, doing my best to constantly move. Maybe that's why my parents didn't want me."

He watched her for a moment, but then he said something that made her heart soar. "We want you."

Both boys nodded. "We like you!" Sam said.

"I like your stories," Ethan said.

They were such sweet boys that she wanted to kiss them both right then. "Thank you!" she said, tears filling her eyes. She couldn't imagine loving this little family of hers more than she did at that moment, and she'd only met them two days before!

When the meal was served, Amelia looked down at the steak. She watched Anthony as he took his first bite, cutting off a small piece, so she did the same.

She suddenly understood why he'd thought she should try steak right away. It was delicious. "I need to learn how to cook this," she said, smiling happily as she cut off another bite of the meat.

"Most people just fry it," he said.

"Well, I like it." She looked over at the boys. "Do you like steak?"

They both nodded, as they spooned their chicken and dumplings into their mouths much too quickly for Amelia's peace of mind.

"I'll learn then." She looked at Anthony. "The store is closed on Sundays, right?"

He shook his head. "No, with the railroad coming through here and it being the primary source of business, all of the businesses in town stay open seven days per week. Their Sunday hours are reduced, but everything is still open."

"Could we get some fabric for some new clothes for the boys? I'm happy to sew, but they're outgrowing what they're wearing, and with Sam going to school this year..."

He nodded. "Absolutely. We'll get whatever you need."

"I wouldn't mind more yarn as well. Both boys wear socks that have been darned many times. It would be good if they each had a few new pair."

"Absolutely."

She was so excited she didn't even know how to express it. Now when she joined the family in the parlor in the evenings, she would have work to do and wouldn't feel so lazy and uncomfortable.

After he'd paid, they walked to the store, which was very close. There weren't a lot of places within Midland that weren't in walking distance. The whole town had been built on the railroad, and every business was close to the train station.

She let the boys pick their favorite colors for their shirts, and she bought the fabric to make two pairs of pants for each of the boys, but she chose brown and grey for those. They wouldn't show as much dirt, and the colors would go with whatever color shirt they wanted.

She let them choose their yarn colors for socks as well, preferring to have each boy in a different color so their socks wouldn't get confused.

She added thread, and buttons to her order as well. There. Now she would have things to do in the evening, and the boys would be well dressed for school.

Anthony carried everything to the wagon for her, looking at the large pile. "You're going to be busy for the next year doing all this!"

She laughed. "If I didn't have the garden and canning to think about, it would all be done in a few weeks. But with the garden, I will definitely have it all done before school starts." She looked at Sam. "Are you excited to start school?"

He shrugged. "I don't know."

"Can you read yet?" she couldn't believe she hadn't thought to ask him that.

He shook his head.

"Then I'll teach you. We'll set aside twenty minutes every day, and I'll get both you boys reading in no time."

Anthony helped her into the wagon. "I want to say you're biting off more than you can chew, but I've seen what you can do in a day. Just don't get sick from doing too much."

She laughed. "I'm more likely to get sick from not doing enough. I love to work!"

"Don't think I haven't noticed," he said.

When they got home, she wanted to start cutting out the fabric immediately, planning to use their shirts as a pattern, just adding an inch or two to everything. Instead, Anthony talked her into working in the garden with him. "You've been doing a great job getting everything harvested, but I think we should do it together."

The boys were napping, so she smiled and nodded. With the two of them working together, they were able to finish harvesting the blackberries, having to empty their pails several times into the kitchen.

He shook his head. "I think Mrs. Hamilton may have planted too many blackberries."

She laughed. "You're talking to a girl who was raised in an orphanage. There are never enough sweet treats around to keep me satisfied. I want pies, and muffins, and jam. We're going to have a wealth of canned goods this winter, and we will not run out of sweets."

"It sounds to me like you had a dismal childhood," he said softly.

She laughed. "I lived with all my close friends, and it was truly a glorious way to grow up. I don't think I would have been nearly as happy growing up with parents."

Chapter Nine

A month later, Amelia still loved her new family, though this time she loved them with even more knowledge of what wonderful people they were, which made her love them even more.

All of the blackberries and blueberries had been canned and put into the cellar for later, and she had moved on to harvesting watermelon and corn. Some of her neighbors at church were harvesting grapes and cotton, and she'd made a deal to trade watermelons for some grapes. She loved grape jelly the best. Why, she'd even agreed to give Nancy, the woman who was trading her the grapes some of her grape jelly when it was done.

Late on a Saturday afternoon, Amelia went out to get as many of the ripe watermelons as she could. There was a church picnic the following day, and she planned to take some with her to share and trade. Many of the others in the church had agreed to bring produce to trade.

Amelia would take some of the corn she'd harvested earlier that day, and hopefully, people would trade even more grapes for that. She knew several neighbors raised grapes, and she was ready to take some off their hands.

When Anthony came home, he saw Amelia working in the garden. "I wish you'd harvest only in the mornings," he said for what seemed the millionth time. "It's too hot for you to be out here in the afternoons."

She shrugged. "We're taking some of the ripe watermelons to the church picnic to trade for others' produce tomorrow, and I want to be sure to have them as fresh as they can be." She stood for a moment. "I suppose I could harvest them in the morning."

Anthony shook his head. "How many do you have?"

She pointed to the wheelbarrow, overflowing with watermelons. "But I can't let any go to waste! We have a few families in our congregation who have very little to eat. They can enjoy fresh watermelon! And I can put up watermelon jelly and jam. I've never tried them, but I have a book of receipts for canning, and it says they turn out delicious."

He gaped at her. "You know it's not your job to feed the entire congregation?"

She nodded. "But just think. We have so much corn and so much watermelon. Part of the reason for the picnic tomorrow is to share the produce that we won't use, and we have more than we need."

He sighed. "All right. We'll all come out after supper and get more."

She threw her arms around him and kissed him. "You're the best husband in the whole wide world!"

"I'm going to go get a bath and if the boys aren't up from their nap when I'm done, I'll come help before dinner as well."

Her smile told him everything he needed to know. Mary hadn't been willing to do much, but in turn, she hadn't expected him to do anything when he finished work for the day. With Amelia, he was always involved in some project or other.

She continued harvesting until Ethan came out, and called to her. "Wicked Stepmother! It's time for supper!"

Amelia smiled at the nickname. It made her feel so special. "I'm coming." She wiped her hands on her apron and hurried inside, promising herself she'd get all the laundry done on Monday. All of her clothes were covered in dirt except her church dress, and she would need other clothes to wear as she continued to harvest all she could.

After supper, she helped clear the table, but Mrs. Hamilton told her to go do as much harvesting as she planned to do. It made no sense for her to help with the dishes and be out even later dealing with the watermelon.

Thankfully, the boys were happy to work on the corn, while she and Anthony dealt with the ripe watermelons. She was keeping twenty for herself, but whoever had planted the garden must truly love watermelon. She'd even taken a few to Leslie, who hadn't taken the time to plant her own garden and was happily taking any extras from Amelia, who was there almost daily with more and more of her harvest.

Finally, as the sun was setting, Anthony said, "We need to stop. There isn't going to be room for the boys in the back of the wagon if we keep going."

Amelia laughed. "I suppose you're right."

Anthony chose the biggest watermelon from the wheelbarrow carrying it inside. "Who wants watermelon?" he asked, taking it into the kitchen where Amelia washed it and cut it into slices.

The boys each took huge pieces and Anthony took one as well. He looked at Amelia. "Why aren't you having any?"

She shrugged. "I've never really liked watermelon all that much."

He gaped at her. "So why are you doing all this work?"

"Other people like watermelon. I'm not going to let food go to waste. I'd eat it if there was risk of it rotting, but I'll turn whatever's not eaten into jam and jelly."

"But...why go to that trouble if you don't like it?"

She smiled sweetly. "You and the boys love it."

He sighed. "Do you ever do anything for yourself?"

"I made myself three new dresses, a new nightgown, which you never let me wear, a new bonnet, and a new apron before leaving Massachusetts. I think that's enough doing for myself for a while. Besides, I so enjoy doing for you and the boys. When I sew, it may be the boys who will wear what I make, but I get a great deal of enjoyment from sewing."

"Someday soon, I'm going to take you on a picnic. No boys. Just the two of us. And I'm going to show you it's possible to have fun just for the sake of having fun."

"That's what you don't understand," she said. "I have fun with whatever I do."

He shook his head, wishing he could get her to understand. He'd have to do it later, though.

The following morning, she was so excited about the produce exchange and picnic. No one was supposed to take money, because it should all be trade. She took some of the jams, jellies, and pie filling she'd already put up and many ears of corn, as well as the huge amount of watermelon.

She was so antsy in church that Anthony had to tell her to quit fidgeting. "I'm just so excited," she whispered back.

He nodded. This was the first time their church had done a produce exchange like this, and he was certain she'd had a hand in planning the whole thing.

As soon as church was over, she hurried outside, spreading a quilt she'd found in a trunk in the room she shared with Anthony. Then she took the picnic basket out, smiling as she stroked it. It had always been her dream to own a beautiful picnic basket, and here she was with one that looked like it was straight out of the Sears and Roebuck catalog.

She carefully unpacked the plates, glasses, knives and forks that fit into a special spot in the picnic basket before fixing a plate for each of the boys, one for Anthony, and then one for herself.

She poured water into glasses for each of them, and she planned to cut a watermelon and give slices to whomever wanted them after they had all eaten their fill.

A woman whom she'd never spoken with had set her blanket on the ground beside hers, so Amelia went over to that side of the blanket and smiled. "I'm Amelia."

"I'm Miss Horner, the school teacher. I was hoping I'd get to meet you. I understand Sam will be in my class in the fall."

Amelia nodded. "He will. What all should he know before he starts school? He's reading quite comfortably and I've taught him his addition and subtraction. What else should I do?"

Miss Horner smiled. "No one else bothers with even that much, so Sam will be ahead of the rest of his class."

"Oh, good. I've only been here for a month, but I love those boys so much, and I want to give them every advantage in the world." Amelia eyed the other woman's plate. She seemed to only have a simple sandwich there. "Would you like some potato salad? I'm used to cooking for an entire orphanage, so I made a bit too much. And there's too much ham."

Miss Horner nodded. "I would love some."

Amelia took the other woman's plate and served her a large helping of both. "I'll make sure you get a watermelon to take home as well."

"You're very kind," Miss Horner said.

When they were finished eating, Amelia carefully put the dirty dishes into a burlap sack so they wouldn't dirty up the picnic basket.

Then she set up a small table Anthony had kindly loaded for her, and she set the watermelon atop it sliced it in half, and then sliced it into many pieces of watermelon.

Mrs. Hardy came to her with a huge basket full of grapes. "Oh, thank you!" Amelia said. "Watermelon and corn? Just corn? Just watermelon? I even have some blackberry pie filling and some blueberry pie filling all made up and ready. And some jam. Some green beans already canned. And lots of potatoes."

Mrs. Hardy rubbed her hands together. "If I bring one more basket of grapes, can I choose some of everything?"

"Oh, that would be wonderful! I'm so excited about getting grapes that I just can't tell you how happy this is making me."

"I'll be right back."

A small line was forming for Amelia, and she couldn't be happier. She gave everyone a slice of watermelon, and many people wanted to trade. "I made some strawberry preserves that I would love to trade for watermelon or corn, whichever you want."

Amelia smiled. "If I can have six cans of preserves, I'll let you choose some of everything we have. I've got blackberry pie filling and jam. Blueberry pie filling and jam. Watermelon and corn. Oh, and Mrs. Hamilton and I canned some green beans as well. There's a bit of bacon in them, so I hope you don't mind that. Potatoes too!"

The woman smiled happily. "Let me go get the preserves, and then I will shop your wagon."

"Thank you!" Amelia called to her as she gave watermelon to two more children.

The next family that was there, simply took watermelon, but didn't offer anything to trade. "Did you have a bad crop?"

The woman nodded. "All of ours caught fire. The boys were playing with a magnifying glass too close to the garden."

That was enough to make Amelia leave her spot. She'd brought large burlap bags for this purpose. She took a bag, added three watermelon, then took two more, filling one with ears of corn, which surrounded a few cans of jam and pie filling. Then she put a few cans of green beans in the last bag. She handed everything to the woman who was in front of her.

"I don't have anything to trade."

Amelia thought about just giving the bags filled with produce to the woman, but instead, she said, "I could use some help weeding one morning this week. If you'll help me weed for two hours, you can take all this with my blessing."

Mrs. Wilson had tears in her eyes when she hugged Amelia. "This means so much to me."

"I understand," Amelia said. "I was brought up in an orphanage."

"No wonder you're so generous. Thank you. I'll see you tomorrow morning, right after breakfast."

"I'll look forward to it."

And on the day went. Amelia gave away almost as much as she traded for, and everyone seemed to leave happy. The back of the wagon was full between the things she'd gotten in trade, the boys, and the remains of their picnic.

Anthony looked away from the road at his beautiful wife as he made the short drive home. "You are truly amazing," he said softly.

"We have more than we could ever eat," she pointed out.

"But you could have sold it. It's your sweat that has gone into that garden. I know Leslie helped before you arrived, but you've paid her back many times over in produce already, and I have this odd feeling, you'll give her more soon."

"I feel like we got some wonderful things today, and I'm glad we did this. I have grapes for jelly and maybe enough for a batch of juice."

"No wine?" he asked. Mary had always thought grapes should only be used for wine.

She wrinkled her nose. "When you grow up in an orphanage, you learn from a very young age that alcohol is a sin, so no wine."

"Suits me just fine." He smiled over at her.

When they arrived home, Mrs. Hamilton was there, already working on their supper. It had been a couple of hours since lunch, so Amelia wouldn't complain about eating soon.

Amelia carried in the grapes and set them on the counter in the kitchen. Mrs. Hamilton smiled happily. "We're going to have grape jelly!"

"We're going to have a lot of grape jelly," Amelia said, happier than she should have been. "It's so easy to find people willing to trade for what we have when I want what they have. I love it here!"

Mrs. Hamilton looked at Amelia. "You know this wouldn't have happened without you, don't you?" she asked.

"Oh, I know everyone said this was the first time they'd done it, but everyone was involved."

"Because *you* suggested it and how it should be done, and you put in the work."

"I'm just glad to have more of what we need." Amelia washed her hands. "I'm not going to work on grapes until tomorrow, though. I'm so tired." She shook her head. "Anthony keeps me up long into the night, and it makes my days a bit harder, but I certainly don't want him to die."

Mrs. Hamilton gave her an odd look. "Die? Why would he die?"

"When I asked him what would happen if he didn't have marital relations often, he said he would die. So I'm always available to him so he doesn't die."

Mrs. Hamilton shook her head. "He won't die. I don't know why he would have said such a thing, but men go for long periods without a woman to warm their beds all the time. Mr. Martin went from January until the end of June without."

"I never thought of that." Amelia felt a bit stupid for believing her husband, and even a little upset with him for lying to her that way. She'd thought everything was perfect between them, but not if there was a lie like that hanging over their heads. She would talk to him about it that very night.

Chapter Ten

All through supper, Amelia thought about how to talk to Anthony about what would happen if they didn't have as much sex as they had. She was happy to bring him pleasure, and she certainly got her share of pleasure from what they did, but him telling her he would die without it felt like a terrible betrayal of her trust.

She helped wash dishes after supper, and while she worked with Mrs. Hamilton, she talked about further plans for the garden. "I think I'm going to make watermelon jam and jelly tomorrow. There are still at least twelve watermelons that we harvested that haven't been taken by others or eaten here. There are a few still on the vine that weren't quite ripe, so I can use those as a treat as they become ripe."

Mrs. Hamilton nodded. "There may need to be another trip to town for more jars. You are a canning powerhouse, Amelia."

She smiled. "I do love knowing my family will have treats all through the winter. I have someone coming to help weed tomorrow morning in exchange for the produce I gave her, and then I plan on taking the boys for a walk and we'll pick some apples. I noticed some apple trees here on the ranch, and apples will be perfect for apple pies, jelly, and so many other things."

"All right. But don't wear yourself out. I expect to hear that you're with child any moment, and I really don't want to hear that you're doing too much for that baby."

Amelia nodded. "I'm careful."

After the dishes, she joined her family in the parlor. "Would you mind hitching up the wagon and letting me drive to town on Tuesday?" she asked. "Tomorrow will be all about apple picking."

He nodded. "I can drive you if you'd prefer."

"That would be wonderful." Then she could talk to him about what he'd said while the boys napped in the back of the wagon.

"Why don't you see if Leslie will keep them for the day, and I'll pay her for it?"

"Why?" she asked. She was genuinely curious why he wouldn't want the boys along.

"I think it would be nice to spend a few hours alone with my wife. I'll take you to the diner again, and we'll just have a good day together."

"That sounds nice," she said. It would be easy to have the talk with him without the children. Now things would surely work out.

The following day was Mrs. Hamilton's day off, so Amelia needed to handle all three meals. Thankfully, there was some ham left that she could fry with eggs for breakfast, and she and the boys could have it on sandwiches for lunch. Anthony always ate lunch with his crew on days that he worked.

For supper, she thought she'd bake an apple pie, and maybe even make chicken and dumplings, depending on how much energy she had left after apple picking.

When Mrs. Wilson came the following morning, she had all six of her children with her, ranging in age from six to seventeen. "You brought so many!" Amelia said. "Do you all want to spend the day with the boys?"

"I brought them to help with the weeding. It should be done in no time at all."

"I'm not so sure. The garden is large, and I've only been harvesting with no time for weeding."

"Trust me." Mrs. Wilson sent her oldest to the wagon, and he handed a hoe to each of the other children. "You just sit," she told Amelia.

"Oh, I can't just sit. I do want to harvest some apples today as well, though."

Mrs. Wilson smiled. "Then I'll have half my crew here working on your garden, and the other half will pick apples with you. You've done so much for us, that we will be able to return the favor."

It was so much more than Amelia had imagined. Mrs. Wilson brought three tall boys, who said they'd climb the trees and drop apples to the ground, then all Amelia had to do was pick them up. So while Mrs. Wilson watched over her younger children with the garden, Amelia took her two, and they picked up the apples the big boys dropped. She carried five baskets out to the trees with them to fill with the apples, and every single one of them was filled within an hour.

The boys helped her carry the apples back to the house, and she saw the garden was mostly done. After putting the baskets of apples onto the porch, the boys picked up hoes and got to work with their mother and siblings.

Amelia went into the house and filled a burlap sack with apples, giving the other family half of what they'd just harvested, and she promised herself she would take them applesauce and apple jelly, and part of everything else she harvested all summer.

Amelia went to Mrs. Wilson. "I filled a sack with apples for you and your family, but I can't quite lift it now that it's full. Could you have one of the boys put it into the back of your wagon?"

"You can't give us more! We're here to pay you for what you've already given us," Mrs. Wilson said.

"If your crew will come back on Wednesday and help once more, I can have all the apples harvested, and you are welcome to half. You have no idea how thankful I am for your help!"

Mrs. Wilson called out to the boys who had helped, "Who wants to help again on Wednesday for more apples?"

They all agreed. "We love Ma's applesauce," the oldest girl told Amelia. "It's the best thing ever, and she'll make it if we have the apples."

"Wonderful!" Amelia shook her head. "There's more than I can harvest with the two boys. And there's a lot more than we could ever eat. We can't let them rot on the trees."

Mrs. Wilson looked at Amelia. "It was a good day for our congregation when you joined."

"It was a good day for me as well," Amelia said. "Yesterday seemed to be a huge success. I'm glad to be part of such a warm and giving community."

The garden was finished well before noon. "So, you'll come on Wednesday?" Amelia asked.

"I certainly will. And I'll bring all the helpers. Do you have anything else that needs to be harvested?"

"There's a bit more corn, and some more watermelon," Amelia said, looking around. "The whole garden needs to be watered. That's the main thing right now, and then we'll have more to harvest next month."

"The children who don't help with the apples will water the garden for you. If we're eating out of it, then they can help."

"Oh, thank you! It does hurt my arms so when I have to carry the buckets of water, but I'm so grateful for the produce."

Amelia went into the house much earlier than anticipated. She and the boys had lunch, and then she put them down for their naps. And there was time to do the laundry and make jam.

In one pot, the watermelons boiled to make the jam she was so excited to make, though she wouldn't eat a bite of it. She didn't know why people loved watermelon so much. In a second, she had a chicken boiling that she would turn into chicken and dumplings for the boys' supper. Instead of missing out on their favorite meal when they didn't go to town with her, they would get it at home.

She rolled out a pie crust and filled it with apples, sugar, and cinnamon. Lots of cinnamon. That went into the oven. Following which, she walked to Leslie's house, knowing she needed to be in a hurry.

"I was wondering if the boys could stay with you tomorrow while Anthony and I go to town?" she asked, as she gave the other woman a basket full of apples.

"That would be fine. What are you doing in town?"

"I need more jars for canning. Applesauce is on the agenda for later this week." Amelia rubbed her hands together. "I'm having so much fun canning the produce. Thank you so much for all the work you put into our garden."

Leslie shook her head. "I've gotten a great deal more out of it than I put into it. You are a wonder."

Amelia smiled, raising her hand in a wave. "I have to get back to the apple pie before it burns, but I wanted to ask you! Thank you!"

Back home, she was in plenty of time to get the pie from the oven, and she started to roll out the dumplings. It was a long process to make this for the boys, but she loved every minute of it.

The following morning, she and Mrs. Hamilton made applesauce, and Amelia left the applesauce for Mrs. Hamilton to can on her own.

Amelia and Anthony left around eleven for their drive to town. She knew it was supposed to be a special day for her and Anthony, and she was quiet as she tried to find the right words to say to Anthony.

"I know you lied to me," she finally said, and as soon as the words were out, she knew they were wrong.

He gave her a questioning look while shaking his head. "I've never lied to you. I wouldn't."

Amelia looked down at her hands. "Mrs. Hamilton told me you wouldn't really die if we didn't make love quite so often."

Anthony stared at her for a moment and then remembered what she was talking about. "I was joking when I said that. I thought you knew!"

As soon as he said the words, she forgave him. "I knew there had to be an explanation," she said. "You've never done anything that would upset me other than that, and it made no sense to me that you would lie about that one thing."

"Have you only been willing with me because you thought I would die?" he asked, looking concerned.

She shook her head. "No, that's not the only reason. I enjoy what we do. Sometimes I'm a little too tired, but I'll start telling you that now that I know you'll be all right. I do love you, and I love making love with you, but knowing I can take a night off from time to time is nice."

Anthony sighed. "I didn't realize you thought that. I'm so sorry. I would never deliberately deceive you."

"I didn't think you would, which is why I was so bothered."

He put his arm around her after transferring the leads to one hand. "I love you, Amelia. You are exactly what we needed when I sent that letter. I wasn't sure at first, because you're always so...happy. But now that I've gotten to know you, and seen you with my boys... I'm so happy you were the one to come here and be my wife."

Amelia smiled. Of course, she'd known he'd fall in love with her, but it was nice to hear him say it. "I can't wait to write our matchmaker and let her know she made another perfect match."

He grinned. "Have you written the matron yet?"

"Oh, of course. I brought a letter for her to mail while we're in town."

"Good," he said. "But for today, we're going to have a romantic meal, and we're going to get the supplies you need."

"Sounds like a perfect day." She looked up at him, smiling. Anthony was everything she'd hoped for when she read his letter and more. Life couldn't get any more perfect.

Epilogue

Mrs. Wilson served as her midwife a year later. Amelia worked hard to not shout or do anything to make Anthony upset. She was happy to be birthing his child.

"One more big push!" Mrs. Wilson said, and Amelia complied, so happy to hear the baby cry. "It's a girl!"

Amelia immediately wept. "A girl. I have a daughter!"

"You do," Mrs. Wilson said. She gave the baby to Mrs. Hamilton so she could finish up with Amelia. "You need to stop pushing."

Amelia frowned. "I can't!"

A few minutes later, there was another child born. "Another girl."

"Twins?" Amelia asked, feeling a bit dazed.

Mrs. Wilson laughed. "Twins. My first set of twins I've ever delivered."

"But...I didn't know there were two!"

"I didn't either." After a short while, Mrs. Wilson said," You're as presentable as you're going to be. Do you want to hold your daughters?"

Amelia nodded. "And I want to see my family."

"You did great," Mrs. Wilson said as she slipped out the door, giving Amelia a moment alone with the babies.

Less than a minute later, Anthony came back into the room with both Sam and Ethan beside him. They hadn't been told about the twins, so Anthony stopped and stared for a moment. "I should have known you would have to have two."

Amelia grinned. "Aren't they beautiful? Both girls."

He sat down on the side of the bed to look at the babies. "Boys, do you see your sisters?"

Sam came closer to look, but Ethan just stared from across the room. "Don't you want to see them?" Amelia asked.

Ethan shook his head. "Sam said that if I got too close, they'd poop on me."

Amelia laughed, so glad everything was normal with her family. "They're both wearing diapers. They can't poop on you!"

Ethan walked toward the bed slowly, as if he was afraid one of the babies would explode. "When will they talk?" he finally asked.

"Not for a long time yet."

"Oh," Ethan said.

"Okay, time for you boys to sleep," Anthony said. "You can see your sisters tomorrow."

"And our wicked stepmother?" Sam asked.

"I'm here for you always," Amelia said, grinning at her boys.

When Anthony came back into their room a short while later, she was nursing them both. "I'm so happy I could burst," Amelia said. "Thank you for my babies."

He shook his head. "I had the fun part. You had to grow them!"

"Our love grew them," she told him.

He nodded, kissing her forehead. "They're perfect. And so is their mother."

Milton Keynes UK
Ingram Content Group UK Ltd.
UKHW040720161023
430697UK00001B/55